Takasu Ryuuji
SECOND YEAR HIGH SCHOOL STUDENT

W9-DFC-333

Hoodlum. Delinquent. Punk. Mad Dog Takasu. Assailant. Thief. Murderer.

"How scaaary! Those eyes are definitely not normal!"

Say what you like, he's used to being misunderstood.

It's his face. Those eyes; they're hideous. It's just something he was born with, but it's hard getting other people to understand that.

He has one wish: He wants every day to be calm and quiet and clean and safe and orderly.

But, in April of this year, a strange companion came into his life.

Toradora! Digest

Aisaka Taiga SECOND YEAR HIGH SCHOOL STUDENT

Ferocious. Fiendish. She's the best at being the worst. She looks
sweet. She might be tiny, but she's got the spirit of a tiger.

This girl—known as the Palmtop Tiger—destroyed Ryuuji's
quiet way of life. Even though she acts like she runs the house,
he's the one who cooks all the food.

She was abandoned by her parents and has no clue how to do
housework. She was like a starving stray when Ryuuji first fed
her. It wasn't like he wanted it to happen, but, through a series
of circumstances, his cooking tied their fates together in a really
complex way.

Amazingly, the person Ryuuji was in love with, and the person
Taiga was in love with, knew each other.

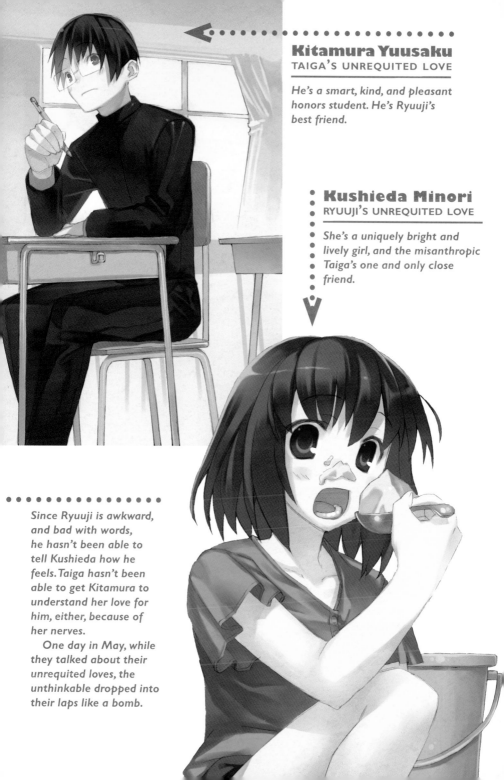

Kitamura Yuusaku
TAIGA'S UNREQUITED LOVE

He's a smart, kind, and pleasant honors student. He's Ryuuji's best friend.

Kushieda Minori
RYUUJI'S UNREQUITED LOVE

She's a uniquely bright and lively girl, and the misanthropic Taiga's one and only close friend.

Since Ryuuji is awkward, and bad with words, he hasn't been able to tell Kushieda how he feels. Taiga hasn't been able to get Kitamura to understand her love for him, either, because of her nerves.

One day in May, while they talked about their unrequited loves, the unthinkable dropped into their laps like a bomb.

Kawashima Ami

On top of her mom being an actress, she's currently a high school model. She's a childhood friend of Kitamura's and an off-season transfer student.

"She's so cute and kind, just like an angel!"

"Ami-chan, you're really clueless, aren't you~"

"But it's cute that she's an airhead."

"Even though she's so pretty, she still has a nice personality!"

"You're too kind! You praise me too much."

Just kidding.

Nobody would praise the true Ami. She's twisted, super mean, selfish, hurtful, and cruel, but no one knows that. Frankly, Ami is terrifyingly two-faced. The good girl mask she wears is hard as iron.

But Taiga's seen through that and they've become enemies. Every time they see each other, they bristle and bicker. Some days, they use their fists and it gets pretty bloody.

Nobody knows what gave Ami the idea, but for some reason she thinks clinging to Ryuuji and saying, "Ta-ka-su-kun ♥" in a flirtatious voice will annoy Taiga.

Every chance she gets, she gets close to him and tries to entice him with her sweet voice... W-wait isn't that going too far?! Hey, people will get the wrong idea!

Toradora!
VOLUME 3
story Yuyuko Takemiya
illustrations Yasu
NO WAY.

Oooh, and here is the masked Kawashima!
She's falling on Takasu, the athlete!
What's the Palmtop Tiger going to do?
Will she join them?
Or will she kill Takasu, the athlete?
How bald will Inko-chan get?
What will happen?
The match continues on the next page!

Toradora! 3

BY

Yuyuko Takemiya

ILLUSTRATED BY

Yasu

Seven Seas Entertainment

TORADORA! Vol. 3

© YUYUKO TAKEMIYA 2006

First published in Japan in 2006 by KADOKAWA
CORPORATION, Tokyo. English translation rights arranged
with KADOKAWA CORPORATION, Tokyo.

Seven Seas books may be purchased in bulk for promotional,
educational, or business use. Please contact your local
bookseller or the Macmillan Corporate and Premium Sales
Department at 1-800-221-7945, extension 5442, or by
e-mail at MacmillanSpecialMarkets@macmillan.com.

Follow Seven Seas Entertainment online at
sevenseasentertainment.com.

TRANSLATION: Jan Cash & Vincent Castaneda
ADAPTATION: Lora Gray
COVER DESIGN: Nicky Lim
INTERIOR LAYOUT & DESIGN: Clay Gardner
PROOFREADER: Jade Gardner, Kris Swanson
DIGITAL MANAGER: CK Russell
PRODUCTION MANAGER: Lissa Pattillo
ASSISTANT EDITOR: Jenn Grunigen
LIGHT NOVEL EDITOR: Nibedita Sen
EDITOR-IN-CHIEF: Adam Arnold
PUBLISHER: Jason DeAngelis

ISBN: 978-1-626929-38-8
Printed in USA
First Printing: November 2018
10 9 8 7 6 5

ToC

Table of
Contents

I*T'S YOUR FAULT.*

A monotone voice that was horribly and unmistakably displeased echoed throughout the quiet hall of the emergency outpatient clinic. It was evening.

"It's your fault... It's all your fault," Aisaka Taiga muttered again hoarsely. She was perched on the right edge of the sofa.

Takasu Ryuuji sat as far away as possible from her on the left side of the sofa, staring at his own toes with his brutally sharp, angled eyes. Saying anything would be futile. He didn't have the strength to fight with her. Besides, this wasn't the time for that.

He cringed as an ambulance passed outside the window, but the siren's loud wail immediately cut off. Only the glare of the revolving red light threw Ryuuji and Taiga's stark shadows on the linoleum floor. It seemed the prestigious emergency room of the college hospital was booming even on a weeknight.

"What time is it now?" Taiga asked, turning to him. Her face was white even in the darkness.

I forgot my watch, Ryuuji thought. He stubbornly didn't meet her gaze and flipped open his phone.

"Just before ten," he answered curtly. That meant it had been nearly an hour since they rushed here in a taxi, and he was exhausted. When he let out a small sigh, Taiga sighed too, running her fingers roughly through her hip-length hair.

"It's okay," he said, trying to take her fatigue into consideration. "You can go home ahead of me."

"I must have hit rock bottom if a dog like you is ordering me around. Just leave me alone. You should be careful about commenting on what I do..."

She practically growled, her voice low, as if she were prowling through a jungle, the air thick with blood. Then, after a moment of silence, Taiga cracked the knuckles on her right hand. *Crack, crack, crack.* Her gaze, the same one she'd been angrily turning on Ryuuji for nearly an hour was practically overflowing with contempt.

But when it came to glares, Ryuuji was undefeatable. His beady black pupils glinted like a sword; blueish, shining, and dangerous as he looked at Taiga. In actuality, that was just how his face looked. It was genetic.

"Huh? Then do what you want?" he finally asked, his voice small. No longer able to stand sharing a seat on the sofa with such a ferocious beast, Ryuuji quickly stood up.

"Hmph." Taiga's snort was arrogant as she shuffled over to the center of the sofa. Then, queen-like and cold, she stuck out her small chest and turned up her chin.

Even at a time like this, she was still the ruler of the carnivores—a ferocious and wild tiger.

Taiga had a small, beautiful face with attractive features and soft, smoky-chestnut hair that spilled down her back. She wore a flower-patterned dress with lace and frills that overwhelmed her tiny frame. She looked too small to be a second-year high school student. Taiga looked startlingly delicate, like a sweet French doll, dainty and pure as a rosebud. Unfortunately, that rose was secretly poisonous. Or rather, it jettisoned poison in all directions around it.

This brutal, ferocious, and cruel girl was also known as the "Palmtop Tiger."

Through various, miraculous events, Ryuuji was somehow basically living with her.

"Haaa..." Ryuuji stooped and rubbed his eyes with his hands. The situation really had taken a terrible turn.

Although Ryuuji's life had been strange, at least it had been calm. Now, everything was tense and turbulent. After rushing to the hospital in the middle of the night, he was at a loss. He could only stand still and stare intently at the examination room door as they waited in the dim hallway for the doctor to appear. Time marched on, but they still had no idea what was happening or what treatments were being administered within the examination room, nor how grave the situation actually was. As the silence between them stretched, disturbed by the sound of their breathing, the worry in the pit of Ryuuji's stomach grew.

"I wonder what'll happen..." Taiga mumbled. She sounded tired and unhappy but wouldn't go home. She was probably as uneasy as Ryuuji. Despite what she'd said earlier, she likely felt it was her fault, too.

What's going to happen? Really? Ryuuji thought. *If something happens—no way.* He didn't even want to think about it. He closed his eyes and shook his head, trying not to think about the worst-case scenario.

Then it happened.

The examination room door opened. "Takasu-san, please come in."

Ryuuji's head snapped up at the voice. "D-doctor! What's happened, what's wrong?!"

"For the time being, just come inside."

Ryuuji burst into the examination room, flinching momentarily at the brightness. The moment the harsh ring of light faded, Ryuuji saw the member of his family weakly stretched out on the table.

"It... It can't be..."

That silent body showed no signs of warmth or life.

Taiga, who followed in after him, caught her breath and took a quiet step back toward the wall.

The doctor gently touched Ryuuji's shaking shoulder and pointed to the fallen body. "Pretty ugly mug it's got there." The doctor's finger poked the pitch-black beak, and the ash-blue parakeet tongue lolled out. "It's alive."

A silent moment passed.

"H-huh?!"

"No way?! She's got to be dead! Look at that!"

Taiga's words earned a shake of the head from the doctor, the veterinarian. "It's alive. It doesn't have a single thing physically wrong with it."

Still in disbelief, Ryuuji stepped hesitantly toward the Takasu household's cherished pet, Inko-chan. She lay face up on the exam table. Her twig-like legs were so messily entwined, he couldn't tell what was going on with them. Her mouth was slack in a way that made him want to censor it, and her wide-open eyes were completely white. Her wings were half-open and ruffled, and there was a string of some unidentifiable liquid coming from the end of her beak. Furthermore, her feathers, which had been falling off in droves, but at least covered her whole body when they brought her in, were missing in spots, making her look bald and patchy.

"I-Inko-chan? It's me. Do you remember me?"

"..."

"Inko-chan! If you're alive, answer me! Say something!"

"..."

But Inko-chan remained creepily splayed out like a corpse and didn't answer. Ryuuji could only detect a heavy sense of rigor mortis from her.

"Doctor! She's not answering!"

"I don't think a parakeet normally would."

"Inko-chan does though!"

Ryuuji turned to the veterinarian with his dangerous eyes, and the veterinarian silently averted her gaze, taking three wide steps away from him. *What kind of person is she,* Ryuuji wondered. Actually, come to think of it, she had just called his pet ugly.

Though Ryuuji was normally gentle, he couldn't help feeling annoyed.

"Move over a little." Taiga brushed past Ryuuji's shoulder and stepped straight up to the examination table.

"There's nothing physically wrong with her. She's faking it, right?" Taiga asked. She looked down at Inko-chan's odd, unconscious form and quietly checked her over. Inko-chan's profile was obscured by Taiga's hair.

"T-Taiga? Wait a sec. What are you trying to do?"

"She's pretending. She's faking it. We were so worried and spent two thousand yen on a taxi, and she's faking it. That's weird. Right, Ryuuji? It's hilarious."

But Taiga sure wasn't laughing.

"Hmph. If you're going to insist you're sick," she said, "at least put your heart into it. Huh? You ugly bird."

That's when Ryuuji saw it.

Inko-chan, who had been firmly motionless, had a sudden eye twitch. Taiga must have also seen it, but it seemed she intended on following through.

"Say, do birds have spines?" she asked, her voice reverberating sinisterly.

"No," the veterinarian said. "Even though there isn't anything wrong with her physically, that doesn't mean she's faking it. Basically, it's a psychological issue."

"Should I go from the top? Or the bottom?" Taiga pressed, purposefully ignoring the veterinarian.

Ryuuji hurried to stop her. Then, before his eyes, Inko-chan began to tremble faintly. Liquid bubbled up from her beak.

The bird had broken out into a cold sweat.

"Inko-chan!" Ryuuji cried. "If you're going to wake up, you've gotta do it now!"

"Ryuuji, keep to yourself! This ugly child takes advantage of us because you spoil her! I'll slap that ugly attitude out of her!"

The voice of Inko-chan's owner bellowed in desperate futility as Taiga's small hand cut through the air—then, in the next second, it happened.

"I CAN FLYYYYYYYYY!"

"Oh, she flew."

Or rather, she jumped. Maybe. Inko-chan, who had been unconscious, let loose a strange cry. *Shping!* Her back recoiled like a spring as she jumped high in the air. *Whoa!* Before her owner's wide eyes, she overshot and hit the ceiling.

"Ahhh! I-Inko-chaan!"

She awkwardly crashed onto the floor.

"This is terrible!"

Flustered, the veterinarian rushed over and gently flattened Inko-chan, picking her up to check for injuries.

"Ugh!" After seeing the parakeet's face, the veterinarian re-coiled again. Possibly noticing Ryuuji's critical eyes, she quickly recomposed her professional face and examined Inko-chan's body for abnormalities.

"She's fine," she said. "She's not hurt in any specific way, but... but...this parakeet is utterly repulsive. Where did you get her? I can't believe anyone would sell something like this. This *is* a parakeet, right?"

Then, to add insult to injury, she said, "Can I take a picture? My daughter loves this sort of weird stuff. She's only six, but she has an entire collection of grotesque pictures."

"Isn't that something you should be more concerned about?"

"You think so?" the unconcerned veterinarian asked as Ryuuji snatched his beloved pet from her hands. He gently held Inko-chan to his chest.

Inko-chan really was ugly but doubting she was a parakeet went too far. Reducing her to a "grotesque" photograph was terri-ble. He'd never come to this veterinarian again if he could help it.

They were at the university hospital's prestigious emergency room's...neighbor.

This was the place that, after feverishly flipping through the yellow pages and calling each place in turn, they had finally set-tled on. It was a large hospital for animals and one of the few that offered nighttime emergency care.

"Well, anyway, we're lucky it wasn't a horrible disease. Right, Inko-chan?" Ryuuji's glinting eyes looked like he was a moment away from devouring his prey as he gingerly stroked Inko-chan's head. He wasn't planning on eating Inko-chan alive, starting with her noggin—he was cherishing her.

"Nko-chan, Nko-chan, Nko-chan, Nko...nnn...uuuh...nko."

"Yeah, yeah, that's right." He put his mouth up to her ear...or rather, to the side of her head where he thought her ear might be. "That was close. Just when we found out you weren't sick, Taiga almost took you out. She was close to bringing you down. Seriously, I wish she wouldn't vent her anger like that."

"*What?*"

"You heard that?" He thought he'd whispered so only the bird could hear.

"I heard it, all right. Who are you saying is venting her anger?"

Taiga, who had above average hearing, gave in to her frustration and punched the examination table with a *BAM!*

"W-w-w-wait, what're you doing?" Ryuuji asked.

She was also an above average klutz. The force of the punch, one a normal person would have anticipated, had flipped over the tray of medical instruments. Everything fell to the floor.

"Those were sterilized! If you keep going like that, this parakeet's never going to get better. She's really stressed out!"

As Taiga picked up the fallen instruments, the tired-looking, on duty veterinarian compared Taiga and Ryuuji's faces.

"You always fight like this, don't you?" the vet asked. "Pets are surprisingly sensitive. There have been cases where the pet's physical health fails because it senses its owner is stressed."

I see, Ryuuji thought, averting his gaze.

"But we're not fighting," he said.

Taiga suddenly spread her arms, snorted, then laughed scornfully at the veterinarian's words. "I was just 'correcting' this perverted, foul-eyed dog. He's a liar and delusional. I guess I could have ignored him, but I'm too cultured to endure something like that."

Ryuuji couldn't stay silent.

"Huh? I wasn't lying," he said. "Seriously, don't take it out on people weaker than you just because you didn't like what happened."

Maybe saying that was "rash." Maybe it was "foolhardy." In any case, he really should have kept his mouth shut.

"Huuuuuuh," Taiga said. "So in the end, you can't stand being corrected? Is that it? You should be grateful. Hmmmmmm. In that case, how about I spell it out for you? What exactly am I supposed to be 'taking out' according to you? Huh? I *wonder* what it could be? I can't think of *annnythiiing* at all, can you?"

The Palmtop Tiger's eyes glinted as though she wanted to use the tips of her claws to toy with her prey before she killed it.

Ryuuji held his breath. He would be in hot water whether he backed off or attacked.

He chose to attack.

"If you've got something to say, just say it!" he shouted. "Pouting and being annoyed all the time is just rotten behavior!"

There was a moment of silence.

In that hush, Taiga slowly put her right hand to her right ear and deliberately turned to Ryuuji's mouth. Then she stuck out her chin in exaggeration and put her left hand on her hip. With that pose, she made an incredibly simple interjection, "HAAA?"

Can't hear you, can't understand you, not that interested anyway... There probably weren't many people in the world who could express that so spectacularly with such a nuanced, half-faced jeer.

"Y-y-you..." Desperate and directionless, Ryuuji's conviction left him.

Taiga raised her chin in contempt, and despite the thirty-centimeter height difference between them, she looked down at Ryuuji. "You know, Ryuuji," she said haughtily, "I'll give it to you straight: I don't have the time to waste on the delusions of a lying, lazy dog like you. Remember this the next time you open your mouth. First, is it something I need to know? Second, will it make me happy? Third, will I care? You got that?"

"Wh-what's there to get, you idiot?! What delusions?! You *are* annoyed and in a bad mood and venting your anger! That's all true!"

"Is that so?" *Hmph.* Taiga lowered her voice. Her eyes glinted strangely as the corners twitched up to a point where they looked as though they might split. Her pupils narrowed to points, as if logic and reasoning had abandoned her.

This is bad. Terror clenched Ryuuji's stomach. If he had been superstitious or faint-hearted, Taiga's look alone would have struck him dead twice.

Then, even more frighteningly, with a voice trilling like a quiet Hamon drum, she said, "You think I'm in a bad mood? I'll show you a bad mood."

Like the hand of death knocking at his door, Taiga's pale hand seized Ryuuji's tongue, holding it with the tips of her fingers.

"Ngh!"

"There's a reason I'm in this mood. Just one reason. It's because you always have these trashy delusions. It's because you keep accusing me of things that I'm so annoyed."

"Owowowowowowow! Y-you'll pull it out!"

"Let it come out!"

Ryuuji held Inko-chan to his chest as his tongue was yanked. The parakeet was being jostled up and down, left and right, and her feathers were falling out in tufts.

"Please go home," the concerned veterinarian wailed in a small voice.

The same conversation had already been repeated over and over again five hours ago.

You're in a bad mood.

I'm not.

Then why are you annoyed?

I'm annoyed because you say stupid things like that.

It was all because Ami had been teasing Ryuuji.

Ryuuji wasn't gullible enough to believe it was anything other than teasing. The bad joke had taken him by surprise as it unfolded that evening in the quiet two-bedroom apartment, but he hadn't consented to any of it.

Takasu Ryuuji and Kawashima Ami—if you skipped the details—had looked like they were all over each other by the window. She had pushed him down onto the tatami mats and was half on top of him.

His mother, Yasuko, who witnessed it first, didn't think it was funny at all. She had dropped the shopping bags in both of her hands and said something to her son. Ryuuji had barely heard her.

"No way..."

What he *did* hear came from behind Yasuko.

Taiga's clear voice came from the front entrance, where she was being carried on his close friend Kitamura's back. She had been covered in mud and looked preoccupied.

Taiga and Ami are natural enemies, and she's definitely going to misunderstand the position I'm in with Ami. This is bad, Ryuuji had thought. *The tiger is about to unleash her wrath.*

Taiga wouldn't just stop at insults. After snapping, there was no doubt she would demolish the apartment. She might even actually kill him this time; there was a reason Taiga was called the Palmtop Tiger, after all. He didn't doubt she had the potential to easily commit such atrocities.

"I-It's...not what it looks like," he said, pushing Ami aside to sit with his legs folded beneath him. His voice caught in his throat, apologetic and pitiful. He had acted like a man caught in an affair. He shouldn't have said anything at all.

Taiga, her eyes wide, had looked back and forth between Ryuuji and Ami. Of course, Ami hadn't offered an explanation for Ryuuji's sake.

"Huh? Is there something wrong? Did I have bad timing?" she had whispered as if they weren't actually in a bind. "Tee-hee ♥."

"Ummm, ummm." Yasuko, seemingly trying to desperately grasp the situation, was wringing her hands. "Ummmmmm." The already loose screws in her head may have all fallen out as she tried too hard to calculate what she was seeing.

Then, Kitamura made his move.

His face blank, he backed up...and retreated with Taiga on his back. He was still muddy from falling in the gutter, and his glasses were askew. He retreated outside, disappearing from Ryuuji's vision, or so Ryuuji thought.

"HMPH!"

Taiga took her hands off Kitamura's shoulders and grabbed the top of the doorframe. Then, like the claw in a claw crane, she wrapped her legs around his hips and pulled, firmly holding him back.

"A-Aisaka! Wait..."

"Kitamura-kun, why are you running? Weren't you going to use Ryuuji's shower? You don't have any reason to run, right?"

Tsk. This being Taiga, she had to have been using the utmost care as she wrenched Kitamura around. Using the terrific strength of her outstretched hands, she suspended her body in the entryway. Then, pumping her knees forcefully, she landed a spectacular touchdown.

"Ah—uhm, Taiga-chan, according to my calculations, ummm, Ryuu-chan is, uhhh...a-a-ah..."

Her braless boobs swinging, Yasuko writhed in agony.

Taiga stalked past Yasuko and toward Ami and Ryuuji, sitting side by side. *Eek.* Ryuuji gulped. Her hair, smeared with mud from the gutter, was plastered to her face. The single eye peeking from beneath that hair was cool as inlaid marble, cool as a killing machine, as she looked back and forth between them.

Taiga stopped directly in front of them. The side of her face tensed.

"Takasu Ryuuji is mine! Don't touch him!" she shouted.

Everyone gulped nervously.

"That's what you *thought* I would say, right?" Taiga continued, her glassy eyes relaxing.

Ryuuji was speechless.

Ami, as expected, played dumb. "Huh? You're not going to say that? How weird... Just kidding!"

She had said *that* in this situation. Ami's courage was real, at least.

"Hmph. Of course I wouldn't," Taiga said. "Too bad, Kawashima Ami. Sorry, but I have no interest in who this pervert hooks up with or how." She laughed sarcastically at Ami. It seemed she didn't even intend to turn a contemptuous look on Ryuuji.

Instead, Taiga simply turned right around. "Go ahead, take your time. I'm going home. Kitamura-kun, I didn't tell you earlier, but my condo is actually really close by. You brought me here, but I'm going to use my own shower."

And she walked straight out of the Takasu house without giving Kitamura a chance to respond.

After that, Ami had fluttered her lashes as she fabricated a pack of lies. "My contact lens shifted, so I was having Takasu-kun look at it."

Yasuko and Kitamura seemed to accept it for the time being, and after taking a shower, Kitamura had escorted Ami back home. Somehow, it seemed to have ended peacefully.

The peace unraveled when Taiga came to eat dinner "as usual."

The trigger was Yasuko.

"Isn't it a relief, Taiga-chan? I thought what happened today would have bugged you, and you wouldn't come for food," Yasuko jabbered as she prepared for her night shift.

Then it happened.

Taiga grinned and firmly turned her face to the TV. "Of course I came," she said. "Why wouldn't I? That's weird. How funny. Nice joke. I wonder what on earth would be bugging me?"

Even Taiga wouldn't take out her anger on Yasuko, the head of the Takasu household.

"Oh, right. No way, I compleeetely forgot," Yasuko said. "Come to think of it, Ryuuji, you did something incredibly naughty today, didn't you? Hah! I don't care about that. More importantly, what's for dinner tonight? Oh, is it takikomi rice? Huuuh, but it would have been better as red bean rice. Ha ha ha."

With one hand on her hip and the other over her mouth, Taiga turned her back and laughed. But her eyes weren't laughing; they weren't laughing at all. They were wide, seething, and very annoyed.

I definitely need to explain myself, Ryuuji thought as he prepared food in the kitchen. Of course, he hadn't actually done anything wrong, and, even if he had, why should Taiga tease him or get so prickly?

"Um...Taiga?"

The girl named Taiga was also the Palmtop Tiger, and she wasn't the type to quickly get over her anger when something displeased her. Being friendly with Kawashima Ami was enough for her to give him a guilty verdict.

In that case, let's keep an eye on the tiger.

"Aaaaaah, do whatever you want! Hey, ugly bird! Ha ha ha!" Squatting down, Taiga held Inko-chan's birdcage in both hands, anger crackling blue sparks from her back.

Whatever. Taiga had already snapped.

Regardless of whether he believed he had done anything wrong, Ryuuji knew he needed to apologize to preserve peace in the house.

"Taiga, hey," he said, stepping toward her and poking her back. *"What?"*

Her laughter ended abruptly. The only sound that remained in the Takasu house was Yasuko's hair dryer.

"How do I put this, um, about that thing that happened in the evening..."

"What *thing*? I don't know what you're talking about."

Taiga's back was still turned to him coldly, and he faltered. "Kawashima was teasing me. Well, I think you know that, but I, at least... How do I say this... It seems like it made you upset. Sorry."

"Eek..."

The cry came from Inko-chan. Ryuuji couldn't see Taiga's face, but the parakeet was looking up at it. Inko-chan stepped back, falling off her perch.

"Why are you apologizing? You're so weird, Ryuuji. Oh, right, today I want to watch the ugly bird while I eat. Bring it here."

With her back still facing him, Taiga requested her bowl by stretching out her arm. Inko-chan was still the only one who could see her expression.

"Wh-what are you going to do about the side dishes? It's baked fish. Alfonsino fish..."

"Put it on the rice with the broth on top," she said. "Use a donburi bowl instead of a rice bowl."

After he did that, Taiga ate her dinner without another word, her back to the table. Yasuko and Ryuuji, unable to make conversation, also ate in silence.

"T-time for me to go to work," Yasuko said. It wasn't quite

time for her night shift to begin, but by that point, she wanted to escape.

Which just left Ryuuji and Taiga. Taiga seemed intent to linger at the Takasu house "as usual." The TV offered the only sound in the home. Taiga was staring firmly at Inko-chan and didn't move.

Holding his breath, Ryuuji stood up quietly with the birdcage under his arm.

"..."

Taiga looked up wordlessly at Ryuuji, her eyes reduced to gleaming slits.

"Uh... I need to put the cloth on Inko-chan," Ryuuji said. "She has to sleep soon."

"Why? Don't you usually do it later than this?"

"W-well... Inko-chan looks tired."

"I want to keep looking at her. Leave her here."

Taiga grabbed the birdcage from below. It tipped, spilling Inko-chan's water.

"Why?" Ryuuji asked. "You never want to look at Inko-chan."

"What? Is that bad? Is that weird? Does it bother you?"

The two of them fell silent, still gripping the birdcage.

"*Fine!*" Ryuuji finally exclaimed. "I get it. I get it, okay. Just give me Inko-chan for now."

Taiga's eyes narrowed. "What do you mean, 'you get it?' What? What is it? What are you trying to say?"

Inko-chan's birdcage had been suspended between them the whole time. The air in the room felt cold.

"Ah, no, I just... I get that you're angry, is what I meant."

"That I'm *angry*? Me? Does it look like I'm angry? Why? Maybe you want to say something like this: 'You're jealous because you caught Kawashima Ami and I being naughty.' Are you saying you have to apologize because I'm *jealous*? That you're *that* important? That I'm so pitiful I have no choice but to be overcome by jealousy?"

Taiga slowly stood and took a step forward. Holding the birdcage to his chest, Ryuuji backed away instinctively but immediately hit the wall (the downside of a thirty-eight square meter living space).

"C-calm down," he said. "That's not what I meant. I just want to live peacefully, like normal."

"You didn't mean that? Haven't you been saying this whooooole time that I'm always upset and angry? According to you, this is normal for me. Weeell, fine. I'll get angry. That's easy. I fell into a gutter, scraped my knees, and it reeked so bad I wanted to cry—it was the worst. I didn't want Kitamura-kun to ever see me like that, but he found me, and he carried me on his back even though I stank. And the whole time you were fooling around with that detestable girl. With *her*."

As she stepped closer, Taiga wrinkled her nose like a predator. She had a firm glare on Ryuuji. Her eyes now burned with the bright fire of anger, and her pale lips were twisted into what only looked like a sweet smile.

"But what I hate even more than that," she said, "is you

thinking you know what I want. That you decided I was ashamed. Hey, are you even listening?!"

Like a lover begging for a kiss, Taiga stood on the tips of her toes, her chin raised. In a voice that was colder and more merciless than any other time she had taunted him so far, she added, "Why would I be angry because you're getting friendly with someone? You can wag your tail like a dog at whoever you want. I don't care."

You were mad from the start, though, Ryuuji thought. If he said that or anything else, he'd probably be murdered at this point, even though there were several things he wanted to say. He wisely kept his mouth shut.

"If you value your life, don't say anything that'll make this worse," Taiga said, huffing and giving Ryuuji a contemptuous glance before stepping back, her body no longer pressed against him.

She turned on her heel. "I hadn't minded anything that happened today, but what you said just now irritated me. So I'm going home."

Her sock-clad feet pounded on the tatami as she headed to the front door. Then, it happened.

"One...one...nine..." someone muttered.

"One one nine?" As in the famous Shibuya mall? Oh, no, that's called the "one zero nine." Come to think of it, whose voice was that just now? Inko-chan?

Ryuuji looked incredulously into Inko-chan's cage.

"AAAHHHHHH!" he screamed, because then he understood. One one nine—as in the Japanese emergency number for an ambulance.

Taiga turned, surprised at Ryuuji's scream. "Eek?!" She rushed over, flustered, and pressed her face against the birdcage. "No way. Is it because we were shaking the cage?!"

Inside the birdcage, the pitiful victim who had been caught in the middle of their dispute had shed feathers all around her. She was stiff as a board and had fallen off—possibly fainted off—her wooden perch. Her head was stuck in a gap at the bottom of the cage.

"No way! No way! What should we do?!" Taiga was on the verge of tears.

"We need an ambulance! No wait! A vet!" Ryuuji's voice cracked, high pitched as a requiem.

Takasu Inko-chan would have been six this year.

"What's their problem? That one was empty..."

Staring at the taillights of the taxi as it drove past, Ryuuji muttered, "Damn it." This was the second one.

It had been ten minutes since they left the animal hospital to wait along the national highway. Taxis were already rare here, especially in the middle of the night.

"Are they trying to say they don't have time to pick up high schoolers?"

"Maybe it's because you look dangerous." Holding the small box that contained Inko-chan, who miraculously returned from the land of the dead, Taiga plopped herself on a guardrail and, bored, continued to watch the traffic.

"Whatever," Ryuuji said. "Let's walk to the intersection. I think there'll be taxis coming in from around the station."

Hmph. Taiga sighed as though the idea was tedious and jumped off the guardrail. "Uwah!" She let out a small shriek. A frill of her dress had snagged where the guardrails joined. Frowning, she began yanking at her dress. "Seriously?"

Wrinkles were forming on her brow. Ryuuji quickly stopped her. "You'll rip it! Be gentler!" Kneeling, he lightly tried pulling the frill of her hundred-thousand-yen dress free without damaging it.

"Shut up." Taiga tugged at the dress harder. *Shriiip!* With a high-pitched sound, the thin cotton tore.

After shoving the box containing the bird at Ryuuji, Taiga turned her face away sullenly. Her mood was obvious as she turned on her heel.

"Are you kidding...?" Ryuuji jogged to keep up with Taiga, who was striding down the night street.

"Well, we have some things to reflect on," she said. "We had a pointless fight, and we did something bad to Inko-chan. Hey, Ryuuji—I might have been partly to blame, too, even though you had those stupid delusions about why I was angry."

"Huh?"

Taiga's back was to him, so he couldn't quite catch what she was muttering. Ryuuji finally stole a glance at Taiga's expression when he got to her side.

"I do have some unsocial tendencies." she said, nodding. "So we'll say it's something to laugh about. Because I'm not angry, really. From the bottom of my heart, I dooooooon't caaaaaare at allllll. About you."

"..."

He was too tired to be irritated, or even complain, as he stared at her.

Taiga pushed her hair out of her face as though it were an annoyance, and grinned. "Well then, I'm going first. I don't want to walk with you, you perverted dog."

What a terrible thing to say.

With a plastered-on smile, Taiga turned her back to him and, without a sound, made her way through the misty night. Her posture clearly stated that if anyone disturbed her walking, she would kill them with just a look.

Eventually, Taiga safely caught a cab. Ryuuji wasn't too keen on riding with her just then, but he didn't have much choice.

"Don't loiter!" Taiga shouted.

Ryuuji walked to her as though heading to his own execution, and then got in next to her. Taiga didn't say a word until they finally stopped in front of the Takasu house and Taiga's condo.

She paid him her part of the fare in a practiced manner and went into the condo without a backward glance.

Ryuuji had been planning on paying the whole taxi fare.

Five hours had passed. The situation had only gotten worse.

✦ ✳ ✦

Ahhh, I don't like this.

Where exactly had he gone wrong? He didn't like it; he didn't like it at all. When morning came, he had no doubt Taiga would continue to blame him. When they went to school, he was positive Taiga and Ami would butt heads. Prickling and irritated, their anger would explode.

"No way, no way, no way," he groaned and moaned the whole night, which might have been the reason he couldn't get to sleep.

"Hm...mm? Hm?!"

I didn't hear my alarm go off, Ryuuji thought as he slowly opened his eyes. Then, he looked at the clock.

"Nnnnnnnngh!"

He flung off his towel-blanket and jumped up. The cold reality of seeing the numbers 8:05 cleared his head. Ryuuji's mind raced.

"Oh no, oh no, oh no!"

He had overslept by an hour. At this rate, his perfect attendance was in danger. *First, the bathroom,* he thought as he tried to wriggle out of his T-shirt. He was walking in circles. *What should I do, what should I do?*

"Oh no! Taiga!"

She never woke until he roused her. If he went to her condo to wake her up and make her get changed, they definitely wouldn't make it in time.

He had to do it. At long last, it was time to use the secret weapon. He had stockpiled something for an emergency like this a while ago. Ryuuji pulled a deck brush from its container. As long as he had this, he could wake Taiga.

"Here I go!"

Firing himself up, he opened the window to his bedroom. He kept himself from looking down as he put one foot on the window frame and the other on the boundary wall between him and the neighbor's condo. If he stuck his arms out as far as they could go, the deck brush could reach...

Needless to say, it was Aisaka Taiga's window.

"Taigaaa! Wake uuup! We slept iiin!"

BAM BAM BAM! He hit the glass with the back of the brush but didn't see any sign of Taiga getting up. It couldn't be— she wouldn't have woken up, left him as he slept in, and gone to school, would she? It was possible? Ryuuji hesitated. She was that nasty the day before, and even if he tried waking her up like normal, he didn't know how she would behave. It might be better to just leave her. No, if he didn't wake her up, the situation would probably become even worse.

Oh well, if she isn't there, then she isn't there, and that's fine. This is the last time I'm trying. He once again brought down the deck brush. Then it happened.

"What... ow!"

"Ahh!"

Suddenly, the condo's window opened, and the brush's handle

came down hard on the forehead of a certain sleepy-looking person. Taiga fell straight back and disappeared from Ryuuji's view.

"T-Taigaaa! Keep it together!"

A moment later...

"Ow... ouch..." Clinging to the window frame and pretty much on the verge of crying, Taiga pulled herself up. Somehow, Ryuuji actually felt sorry for her, but they didn't have the time for this.

"S-sorry!" he said. "Wait! We slept in! It's past eight!"

"Huh? Ah...? Why...? Ow... oww..."

Taiga, still half asleep, rubbed her eyes like a child and wiped her nose. She scrubbed the hand that was covered in tears and snot on the belly of her summer pajamas—her pure white, cotton pajamas.

She didn't seem to grasp the situation at all. She buried her face in her long, messy hair. "...What's for breakfast? Why are you waking me up this way today?"

It seemed she had even forgotten to be angry.

"We don't have breakfast or lunch! We're in a hurry, so wash your face and brush your teeth, then put on your uniform! If we don't leave in five, we're late!"

"Nngh...?"

He was lucky she wasn't angry, but he didn't know whether she had understood him or not. She rubbed her eyes once again.

"Ngh." She nodded.

Good, Ryuuji took that as her understanding and then safely landed back in his own room. "Right, hurry up! Close your window! Right! Close it! Lock it, too! Good!"

Taiga's face withdrew, and Ryuuji checked that the window was closed. Then he got about to changing. He realized belatedly that he had been talking to Taiga outside the window in nothing but his underwear.

"I'm really glad she was still half-asleep. Actually, I'm glad no one saw me. Maybe I was half-asleep, too?"

Frantically, Ryuuji put both his legs into his summer uniform pants and quickly buttoned his short-sleeved shirt. He haphazardly brushed his teeth, but neglected his foam face wash, and instead made do with simply splashing himself with water.

He rummaged through the drawers to find socks.

"Ah, Inko-chan and Yasuko need food and water, but I don't have time."

He could only leave a note. He rushed to scribble out something to ask his mother to take care of their parakeet and also herself. Then he did take the cloth off the birdcage.

"Whoa..."

Inko-chan, groggy since returning home from the veterinarian the night before, was still sleeping. Her usual hideous sleeping face, with its spasming white eyes, was enough to shock even her owner. She was still on her wooden perch, her barely-there plumage sparsely fluffed up.

"Sorry about yesterday. Please rest in peace..."

He put his hands together without thinking.

"Inko-chan...is dead? Waaaaahhh!"

Next to the birdcage, stinking of alcohol and having been snoring in her sleep until a moment ago, Yasuko immediately half-opened her eyes. She raised a pitiful cry and, just like that, rolled into a corner of the room.

"*Sniffle...*"

She started snoring once more directly under a dresser.

"H-how could you *say* something like that? She's not dead." Ryuuji didn't think Yasuko could hear him, but he gave her a proper response and gently put a towel-blanket over her. After doing that, he hurriedly put on his socks, grabbed his bag, and ran out of the house.

It was slightly cloudy, but the morning sun was pretty bright. Narrowing his eyes with a mean look, Ryuuji burst through the next-door luxury condo's entrance.

He punched 201 into the auto-locking door's console, worrying there wouldn't be an answer.

"You're so noooooiiisyy!" Taiga wailed quietly as she opened the glass door and ran out.

"So you were awake!"

"You were the one who woke me! My forehead hurts!"

Jerk! She was practically twisting her neck off trying to turn away from him. Anger and contempt dripped from the momentary glance she gave him.

Uwah. It seemed memories didn't fade, even when someone

was half asleep. Even this early in the morning, his spine quaked, but Ryuuji went outside with Taiga.

They dashed under the trees they normally passed and into the grassy scent of the rainy season.

"Taiga, if we don't get to a convenience store, we won't have lunch!"

"..."

"T-Taiga? Did you hear me?"

"..."

"Eek! Don't kick my butt!"

"Don't walk next to me! You're just a perverted dog! I heard you. The convenience store, right!"

"..."

He understood. Whether he was being shouted at or ignored, it seemed that was the only way he would be communicating with Taiga that day.

Taiga's attitude toward Ryuuji was terrible on a daily basis, but somehow this felt much worse than usual. Maybe it was because he had woken her up *that* way. Maybe it was because they had overslept. Ryuuji tried to convince himself of that, but it was clear Taiga's persistent anger was because of what happened the day before.

Hmph! Taiga ardently turned her face away from him once again. Her mouth was firmly contorted as she avoided meeting Ryuuji's eyes.

Aaah... I'm going to be sucked into the same irritation vortex as last night. Even as he had that somber feeling, he heard Taiga mutter, "black nipples," as they ran.

"Huh?!"

"I'm angry about your black nipples. They're burned into my eyeballs!" Her back teeth gnashed as she spat out the words.

The reason she was in a bad mood that day was because of Ryuuji's nipples? Did that mean what had happened the day before didn't matter? If anything, it proved she didn't care about him.

"Th-they're not that dark..."

"They are! The size of your areolas was big enough to fill my retinas!"

What, no way... And so a new form of body image anxiety was born in the sixteenth summer of Takasu Ryuuji's life.

They approached the intersection where Minori normally waited for them, but that day, of course, the goddess who had captured Ryuuji's crumbling heart seemed to have left ahead of time so she wouldn't be late.

"Oh, you finally got here!~ Thanks for everything you did yesterday!"

They ran into the classroom just barely on time.

"Oh dear, did you get bedhead? Did you oversleep?"

The one blocking Ryuuji's path was a beautiful angel who'd forgotten her wings—or rather, the girl who was anything but. It was the nasty Chihuahua, Kawashima Ami. Her large eyes glittered like jewels. She reached toward Ryuuji with a frighteningly white and thin arm that smoothly extended from her summer uniform and then snapped at his hair, which was still sticking up, with the tips of her fingers, as though teasing him.

"Really, Takasu-kun, you're such a sleepyhead!"

She posed as though taking a gravure pinup photo (pursed lips, wide eyes, and stooping over a little to emphasize her cleavage). She smiled perfectly and said, "Cute ♥."

"…"

"Oh dear? What's wrong?"

What's wrong? Ryuuji couldn't help but feel unsettled. He didn't even return a "good morning." It seemed Ami was resolute about keeping up her act in front of Ryuuji. Even after he had seen the dark depths of her true nature, it seemed this girl was still trying to pass herself off as "cute" Ami-chan. This wasn't a joke; he didn't know how she expected him to react.

"Oh, don't misunderstand, okay? Takasu-kun, you're not the cute one, of course. I am! Okay? Takasu-kun, you're always the most wanted one!"

"The most wanted…?"

Ami made a peace sign in front of one eye as she posed.

"Dead or alive ♥."

Slump. He felt as though his stamina was being quickly depleted. A long sigh escaped him. *Yeah, I've got the face for a most wanted poster, all right.*

"You tricked me," he said.

"Hmmm? I wonder what you mean~"

As Ami laughed, he could see the ridicule in her eyes. Where was her firm-as-steel cute girl act? If he looked really closely, he could definitely see the cavernous black eyes of a nasty Chihuahua.

"How are you doing that this early in the morning?" he asked. "Your face will start cramping."

"I'm a pro. I wouldn't mess up that easily." The ill-natured face she rarely showed others returned as she stuck her tongue out just for one moment. She put the mask back on immediately and became a teary-eyed, bubbly, beautiful smiling girl.

"Hgh!"

"You're in the way, dumb Chihuahua."

Ami's unbecoming wail was caused by the corner of the Palmtop Tiger's bag. As the Tiger came into the classroom after Ryuuji, the bag might have just accidentally collided harshly with Ami's lower abdomen as a greeting.

"Oh, oh dear... Aisaka-san, good morning. You seem to be in a really bad mood today."

"Good morning, Kawashima-san. Good job advertising that you're in heat."

Taiga eyeballed Ami and Ryuuji. She gave them a cold look and a sarcastic laugh as she turned to leave.

"Oh, I see~" Ami purposefully laughed loudly and hit her hands together. "You're worried about what happened yesterday, right? That was just a *misunderstanding!* Don't get jealous over something like that. Okay? Envy doesn't suit you, Aisaka-san! Aaah, this is a problem I have. See, I'm oblivious, so I get misunderstood a lot..."

Taiga's feet stopped just then. Slowly, she turned. "You really are an airhead, aren't you?"

The smile that twisted her lips showed her murderous intent. Her words were like a message from the grim reaper; a dark cloud whirled above them.

"About yesterday, it was mere—"

"Heave hup!"

BAM! Taiga ascended into the air. She had finally achieved Super Saiyan flight.

Ryuuji was speechless, his mouth open as a girl with a smile like the light of the sun stuck her head out from under Taiga's armpit before his very eyes.

"Gooooood morning! Taiga and Takasu-kun, you were almost late!"

"M-Minorin...let me down."

The one who had stuck her hands under Taiga's armpits from behind and lifted her small form above her head was Kushieda Minori herself.

"Taiga, you're as light as always," she said. "How do you do it? You eat about as much as I do."

"Don't use me for weight training."

"My upper arms get thin," Minori said as she lifted Taiga up and down. Her smile was perfectly wholesome, the radiant light of a star itself. To Ryuuji, she was the perfect girl.

Her limber body was even more scantily clad now that she was wearing summer clothes. Ryuuji reflexively turned his eyes away, unable to do anything else. After ingesting Taiga's poison the night before, the impact of Minori's cuteness was a little too much. Trying to keep his pulse from fluttering, he averted his eyes. He wasn't angry, he was just flustered.

Ryuuji's appearance didn't seem to bother Minori one bit.

"Come to think of it, Kawashima-san, you're also really thin," Minori said. "Have you been running lately?" She was quick on the prowl, looking for other people's arms to measure their thickness.

Some people might call a situation like this "unrequited love."

Phew. Ryuuji blew out a painful breath. When would Minori finally notice his feelings? She had yet to, though he'd adored her for a while now.

"You two kind of seem lethargic," Minori said. "Did you not have breakfast because you overslept? In that case, you're in luck! I brought these as a snack. Eat this." Minori quickly picked something out of the ziplock bag in her pocket. Ryuuji couldn't tell if she was being thickheaded or sensitive as she said, "Black Nipples!"

She took a raisin in each hand and put them on her bust.

"Eat a boot's worth! Huh? Takasu-kun, why are you so down?"

The one who hit Minori's shoulder in admonishment was Taiga. "Ryuuji is like a traveler who lost his way between his image of himself and the actual truth."

"Oh! That's pretty daunting. You can do it, Takasu-kun! Go for it!"

Minori brought her right Black Nipple gently up to Ryuuji, whose shoulders were slumped. She turned around to put the left Black Nipple firmly into Ami's hand.

"Kawashima-san, I'm really sorry about yesterday!" Minori said. "I regret what I did! I'm the one who came up with the whole plan, but I just had to go to work. I'm sorry. Were you okay? I heard about it from Kitamura-kun, but he said that the stalker extermination was a success?"

"You don't have to apologize!" Ami said. "We were okay in the end! I'm glad, Minori-chan. And thanks. I'll have a Black Nipple, too!"

Next, Minori turned back to Taiga and Ryuuji once again. "Taiga and Takasu-kun, I'm sorry."

"It's fine Minorin, you couldn't help it."

"My apologies." She bent her slender back and bowed her head several times. Her brows furrowed in heartfelt apology. The purity of her gaze when she looked up at him absolved Ryuuji of his anguish about his nipples all at once. He was too nervous for words, but he looked at Minori and desperately waved his shaking hands. *Don't worry about it,* was what he was trying to say.

"Ryuuji doesn't mind at all, right, Ryuuji?" Taiga said.

He nodded. *No matter how much we fight, Taiga still helps me. She really is a good person,* he thought. For a moment, he felt almost cozy.

"So, Minorin," Taiga continued. "It was a good thing for Ryuuji you left when you did. Kitamura-kun and I fell into the gutter and had to abort the mission, but Kawashima-san and Ryuuji got left behind, so he brought her home—"

"Ahhhhhh!"

What was she saying?! Reflexively, Ryuuji tackled Taiga and firmly covered her mouth; but she was prepared and pried off his fingers.

"The two of them were together at the Takasu house. At night. Snuggled up to each other—"

"Why youuuuuu!"

"Black nip—"

Heave hup! He had to silence her! Ryuuji stuck his hands under Taiga's hot armpits like Minori had done and pulled her up with all his might.

"Hey! Let go, you perverted dog!"

I'm not letting go no matter how loud you yell! He flipped her around, trying to get her to go somewhere else.

"Ohhh, Aisaka, good morning!"

"Ah!"

Taiga's nose was practically touching Kitamura Yuusaku, who had cheerfully put up his hand. The strength drained from her body, and Taiga simply went limp. She even forgot to shower Ryuuji in insults.

"G-goo-goo-goo—" Her voice was faint and skipping like a broken record. The heat under her arms jumped by two degrees.

"What's that? It seems you two are playing around like usual."

Kitamura hit Ryuuji and Taiga's shoulders. Ryuuji set her down.

Then Kitamura's eyes went to Taiga. "Here. I completely forgot this and took it home."

"Oh...right..."

"It was splintering a little, so I went ahead and filed it down. Is that okay?"

"Th-thank you..."

Her face went red, and Taiga smiled shakily. Then Kitamura, the class representative whom she was hopelessly in love with, handed her the forgotten object. It was exactly like a scene out of a shoujo manga.

"Don't wave it around too much. It's dangerous."

"Y-yeah."

The thing Kitamura, the dashing hero, handed to the blushing heroine was one frequently used wooden sword. Ryuuji had conflicted feelings about the sword, which had once been used in an attempt to murder him.

"What were you just talking about?"

"Hm?"

Ryuuji turned without thinking, and there was Minori, tilting her head, her clear, brown eyes looking intently up at him.

"What was that Taiga was just saying, Takasu-kun?" she asked.

"Uh, it's not anything, really..."

Of course, he felt like a bomb had begun ticking in his heart. He looked over at Ami for a bit of help, but she had disappeared.

"Ohhh, where did you buy that? It's cute!"

"On the second floor of the station building. It was super cheap!"

"No way! I want one, too!"

"Me, too!"

Far away from him, she was squealing with Maya and Nanako. She was so unreliable. Maybe he was lucky she wasn't there? She wasn't as bad as Taiga, but Ami was a bit of a time bomb herself. A bomb with a mouth on it.

Minori stole a glance at Ryuuji. "Well, because it's you saying it, I'll believe it. Like I said before, if you make Taiga unhappy, then I, Minori, will turn into a beast. Just kidding."

"Oof!"

Slash. Her words were like a knife. Could she have said anything worse?

It was a coincidence that Kitamura said at the same time, "Right, Aisaka? Yesterday, Ami's contact lens got stuck and Takasu was just helping her look at it. That was all. So don't worry about it too much, okay? Don't get mad at Takasu. Stick together!"

"Ah..."

Kitamura's consideration cut Taiga like a knife, as well.

Ryuuji wanted to hold his head. Since they'd met this past spring, nothing had changed about their crushes—except one thing.

Walking together, Ryuuji and Taiga elbowed each other. They exchanged prickling sarcasm, their eyes glinted. Taiga and Ryuuji's relationship was clearly changing for the worse.

"Because of you, Kitamura-kun thinks we're *together!*"

"That's what I was going to say. This is what you get for trying to pull people's legs!"

Twenty-nine and unmarried, this might have been Koigakubo Yuri's lucky day.

"Good morning, everyone!" she said.

She smiled broadly, though her eyes were mercilessly swollen and the double lids she was so proud of were as puffy as tarako roe. None of the students in class 2-C were rude enough to point it out, though one of the other, younger instructors (twenty-seven, with a boyfriend who she claimed she was keeping even though she'd hesitated when he'd proposed the year before) had. *What did she mean by, "Koigakubi-sensei, what happened to your eyes? Shouldn't you do something about them?" What does she know?* Yuri wondered.

"It looks like the weather isn't settling, but I have some good news~" she said.

The night before, she'd gone alone to eat at a family restaurant, (yes, alone). She'd planned on drinking a single can of beer she'd bought at the convenience store but suddenly found she wanted company.

She hadn't seen her childhood friends at all recently. It hadn't been terribly late, so, feeling nostalgic, she decided to call her old friend, Risa, who she had been close to.

Risa immediately picked up and said, "No way, Yuri?! It's been forever! What, no way, let's do something together. This weekend? Oh, I can't do that, I actually have to exchange engagement gifts. Right, right, with that government employee guy. No, it's already past the honeymoon stage, and his parents are so picky now. Oh, Sayaka had a baby! Let's go see them next time we're together! We haven't seen each other since Miho's wedding. How have you been lately? You were dating a younger guy a little while ago, weren't you? Didn't he ask you to go on a trip during Golden Week? What happened with that? Huh? Hello? Hello, hello?"

Don't ask what happened. Yuri thought. *Nothing happened. That's why I didn't mention it. It's not that hard to figure out. Guess!*

Yuri drank three cans of beer; it wasn't enough. She opened a bottle of wine and around two in the morning made some beef kimchi, devouring a heaping pile of salt and calories. By the time she realized what she was doing, she was crying bitterly as she fell asleep.

At 8:30 in the morning the following day, though, she'd managed to pull herself together again.

"The pool will be open starting this week!" she said. "It's a chance to exercise and stay in shape! It's something to look forward to!"

A chorus of "Yay!" and "Bleh!" came from the high school students. The boys were excited and laughing with childish glee. The girls moaned about, "My stomach!" "My fat legs!" "But my arms!" "I can't do a bathing suit!"

Those idiots. Yuri, the matron, sighed. *You're still so young. You don't know how good you have it!*

"Whaaat! This school has coed swimming?!" Ami exclaimed. "No way, that's so embarrassing!"

Kawashima Ami! You're super thin and cute! You're a model! What could you possibly be embarrassed about?!

"Teacher! Let's end homeroom here!"

"All right," she said.

She left it to the overly competent class representative, Kitamura, watching her students absently from her desk as they stood up. At Kitamura's "Stand! Bow!" everyone lowered their heads.

That was when she suddenly realized it. *Aren't I kind of lucky today?*

The most problematic of her students—the Palmtop Tiger, the feared Aisaka Taiga—hadn't so much as irritably clicked her tongue. In fact, the Tiger was obediently quiet. She wasn't exactly being courteous, but she seemed absentminded, and was currently looking intently outside the window.

Taiga's cheeks, which Yuri envied for their rosy smoothness, didn't look like she was feeling unwell, though she didn't seem to be aware of the classroom around her.

Yuri had made it through the morning without the Palmtop Tiger snapping at her. Wasn't that lucky?

Maybe I'll look cute today, too. Maybe I'll have some good fortune. Maybe my marriage prospects will improve... Yuri pumped her fist slightly, fired up for the future.

She didn't notice the ominous cloud of emotion that was beginning to fill her classroom. Maybe she wasn't as good at her job
as she thought.

"I'M NOT ANGRY. Everything's fine," Taiga insisted, already boiling with rage before she had even finished speaking.

Such was the hostility between Ryuuji and Taiga.

Even though she was being vicious and incredibly fussy, Taiga made no moves to cut her time at the Takasu house short. She came for meals, hung around until late, all while being crabby. If Ryuuji tried to explain his actions or ask if she was still angry about the incident, all she said was, "I'm not."

Even mentioning the "incident" had become taboo, and her temper flared every time it was brought up. "Why do I have to be upset over *that*?!" she'd yell. "It's like you want me to be angry!"

I've had enough of this, Ryuuji thought. *What did I do wrong in the first place?*

And then it happened, on a day when Ryuuji was so stressed he thought he was going to have a nervous breakdown.

"Seriously, Taiga, you promised you'd go, didn't you?"

"…"

They had just had finished closing exercises when the Palmtop Jizo statue was born in class 2-C.

"This is the only day I have a break from club."

"…"

Still enshrined in her own seat, the Palmtop Jizo-sama, aka Aisaka Taiga, was as unmoving as a mountain. Her mouth was a sullen, upside down "V."

Kushieda Minori shook her earnestly by the shoulders. "Taiga, c'mon!"

Of course, Ryuuji noticed Minori raising her voice. At any other time, this would be a chance for conversation. *What happened?* It could have been his lucky break, a heaven-sent respite. But after these past few horrible days with Taiga, he couldn't get himself to approach the newly-formed Jizo statue's vicinity.

His interest was piqued by Minori, though, and he gazed enviously at her from afar, his eyes glinting. He wasn't lurking, his teenage heart was just torn between self-consciousness and puppy love.

Then, unexpected reinforcements arrived on the scene.

"Minori-chan, what's wrong?"

Ami, who had finished getting ready to go home, approached Minori and the Jizo-sama and smiled angelically.

Just then, Taiga's Jizo-statue-like facade melted. She bared her teeth as she groaned, "Ugh."

"Stop! That!"

Minori pinched Taiga's nose. Taiga squirmed in pain but surrendered more quickly than expected.

I see, so that's how you tame her. Gotta jot that down. Ryuuji began looking for something to write on.

"Aw, sorry about that, Kawashima-san. I'm completely at a loss with Taiga today. She promised to go swimsuit shopping yesterday at the station, but now she says she won't go."

"Swimsuits? Oh, right, the pool finally opens tomorrow! That's so exciting!"

"Kawashima-san, what are you doing about your swimsuit? Did you already get one?"

"Yeah, I have one I use at the gym. I think it'll work. It's the plain racing type, so it should be fine. It's, like, light gray and there are orange lines on the side and—"

"Oh, that won't work. The school rules say swimsuits have to be plain black or navy and any lines can only be white."

"What! Really?!"

Until then, Taiga had been sitting in her seat and calmly listening to the conversation between Minori and Ami.

"..."

Ryuuji watched.

Taiga quietly grabbed her bag; then she curled, making herself smaller than she already was, and somersaulted from her seat. She quickly slipped by Minori's feet, and, like a beast, dashed away on all fours.

"Ah, she escaped! Takasu-kun, get her!"

"Huh?! R-right!"

Ryuuji grabbed Taiga by the collar reflexively as, by some miraculous coincidence, she tried to run past him.

"Whoa! Good job, Takasu-kun!"

"Let me go, you perverted dog!" Taiga shouted. "How dare you defy your owner, you traitor! You d-d-double-double crossing..."

Aiming to completely ignore Taiga's wail, which doubled the doubles, Ryuuji turned her over to Minori, who had hurried over.

"Thanks for your help!"

"Just doing my duty." Giddy, Ryuuji gave her a playful salute.

Minori turned her attention to Taiga. "Bad TAIGA! Why are you running away?!"

"I-It's not like I promised or anything! You said you wanted to go, so I just said that's fine! I...don't wanna go!"

"Why not?!"

"Because I don't wanna buy a swimsuit!"

"What are you going to do?! Didn't your swimsuit from last year get moldy?!"

Taiga nodded sheepishly.

Ryuuji looked to the heavens. "You've gotta wash and dry swimsuits immediately," he groaned.

"So you have to buy one!" Minori exclaimed. "What are you going to do without a swimsuit?!"

"I'm going to skip all the swimming classes."

"Ouch!"

This time it was Minori's turn to look heavenward. Since he still happened to be standing there, for some reason, she thumped Ryuuji on the back and said, "You're up, sport," with a groan.

He'd gotten dragged into this at some point. As a man, he couldn't ignore Minori's attempt to pass the conversation to him. "If you skip, you won't get a grade for PE," he said.

"This doesn't have anything to do with you!" Taiga glared at him, suddenly overflowing with unexpected (and murderous) enthusiasm.

Ryuuji couldn't retreat in front of Minori; that would be pathetic. Finally, even though it was a little underhanded, he called out, "K-Kitamura! Tell Taiga!"

Kitamura was getting ready to go to the student council room. He paused, his eyes puzzled as he adjusted his glasses. "Hm? What am I telling her?"

"Apparently Taiga's completely planning on skipping all the swimming classes!"

"I can't let that happen!"

"Tsk..." Taiga's face contorted momentarily, mortified, as if she were saying, *Oh no*. But she did have it coming, after all.

Kitamura walked right up to her. "Aisaka, are you not feeling well?"

"N-n-no..."

"Then you have to go to class. Swimming class is mostly fun and games, but school is still school." Kitamura countered Taiga's awkward inability to lie with a fastball of sound logic—the winner, naturally, was Kitamura. "I'm glad you understand! Then I'll see you tomorrow!" As Kitamura waved and left the classroom, Taiga watched him with a hint of resentment.

"Which means it's time to go, Taiga!" Minori said. "Oh, Kawashima-san, why don't you come, too?"

"Huh? But..." Ami's clear eyes glanced at the Palmtop Tiger, who was simmering and seemed to be saying, *I'm already angry, if you come with us I won't forgive you* with her whole body. She looked like she might pull a Dragon Ball and take Flight once more.

"Really, Taiga, what a face you're making!" Minori scolded. "Kawashima-san just moved here and doesn't know which stores sell swimsuits!"

"It's okay, Minori-chan. I'll be fine." With a graceful smile, Ami shook her head, and then hopped back a step. "Because Takasu-kun will accompany me. Right, Takasu-kun? That's okay? Isn't it?"

"What?!"

She entwined her cool, pale arm around his, gently pressing against Ryuuji's elbow. "Can't you?"

"U-uh... Me?!"

She looked up at him with a nod. Although he knew she was hiding her true nature and it was against his better judgement, Ami's pale good looks were still captivatingly gorgeous; almost pure. Against the triple-hit combo of her teary eyes, wobbling lip, and forlorn Chihuahua expression, he couldn't resist. He nodded, knowing he'd been manipulated.

"Really?!" Ami exclaimed. "Yay! I'm so happy, I can really count on you, Takasu-kun~ Oh. You don't mind, right? Aisaka-san." The look she shot Taiga burned with the blue fire of obvious provocation.

"H-huh? What's with the tension?" Bewildered, Minori looked between Taiga and Ami.

Ryuuji couldn't move.

"Why not? So what," Taiga said. She ran her hand through her hair as if annoyed and laughed. Only her rosy lips curved sweetly, even though she seemed like she wanted to spew poison. "Ryuuji says it's fine. That doesn't have anything to do with me. Whatever Ryuuji does with whoever doesn't have aaaaaaaaannn..."

...nnnnnything to do with me, was probably what she would have said.

"OW!"

BAM! There was a dreadful noise as Taiga leaned forward to emphasize her words before hitting her forehead against a desk. The Palmtop Tiger—supposedly the strongest among them—fell to her knees and clutched the lump on her head.

"T-Taiga!" Minori exclaimed.

"Ah, that looked like it hurt," Ryuuji said.

As Ryuuji and Minori checked on Taiga, Ami tilted her head. "Aisaka-san, you couldn't be, like, a klutz?" she asked, her words having lost some of their sting.

She might just have uncovered one of the best-hidden secrets in the world.

"Why?! Why does it end up like this?! You could have gone with Ryuuji to Europe or the North Pole or Demon City Shinjuku or anywhere else!"

"It wasn't on purpose. They say this is the only place that sells swimsuits. Hmmm... Oh, Aisaka-san, this would look great on you. Look, it's for ages six to nine~ It's so cute~ Look, there are frills~"

"Doesn't this look like it'd suit you, Kawashima-san? It's definitely just right for a Chihuahua in heat. Look here, the width's five centimeters."

"Those are boys' speedos!"

"Are they? Then this won't work? Really? The model Kawashima Ami-san on holiday with her pubes fully on display!"

"What're you shouting for?!"

They were in a corner where everyone in the store could hear their fierce exchange.

"I'm so embarrassed."

Ryuuji blushed. It was bad enough he was a high school boy wandering through the girl's swimsuit section, but on top of that, he was in the company of these two.

"Seriously," Minori said. "Taiga and Ami are completely... I'm sorry I got you involved in this, Takasu-kun. It's a little weird."

"No, it's fine," he replied. "I don't mind."

If Minori, glaringly radiant, weren't standing with him in front of the shabby shrubs that decorated the interior of the station building, he would have been at a loss. But because they were together, it wasn't as bad.

It was past four in the afternoon on a weekday evening. Although this was the busiest shopping spot in town, the four-story building was mostly empty. The swimsuit store was particularly desolate, and Hawaiian music echoed sadly in the background.

In that deserted corner of the floor, Minori talked to Ryuuji as she inspected the swimsuits on the rack one at a time. "Takasu-kun, do you have a swimsuit? The men's stuff is behind the pillar over there."

"Yeah. I have mine from last year."

"Right. You would. You're different from Taiga. You wouldn't let yours get moldy."

"Taiga's a special kind of careless."

You're right, Minori smiled in agreement as she took a swimsuit in hand. "Oh, I didn't let mine get moldy, by the way," she said. "I just wanted to buy a new one. So, how's this one?"

Ryuuji wished he were the type of character who would promptly say, "Seems good, it suits you," or something like that. Everything would have gone more smoothly if he had been. Unfortunately, Ryuuji's throat was strangely dry and wouldn't form words.

I'm so worthless, he thought. He hated himself for not being able to embrace this opportunity. He was picking out swimsuits with Minori! It was something he'd only ever imagined doing, and the reality of it was so much better.

Of course, Minori didn't notice Ryuuji's mental anguish.

"Hmmm. How about something that's a little high-cut?" She made a V with her hands and measured the angle of her crotch and then put the swimsuit back on the rack. As she slowly headed to a different display, she said, "By the way, I've thought this forever, but, Takasu-kun, you always keep your uniform and tracksuit super neat. You even iron them properly."

"What?"

Huh... It couldn't be. Was that a compliment?! Although his brain blanked out from the shock, he managed to say, "Y-you think so?" while looking at her profile. "Um, well, my mom works, so I have to do that kind of stuff by myself, but it's not like I don't like doing it..."

"Whoa, that's amazing! So you actually do the housework yourself?!"

His cheeks burned and he turned his face away reflexively. He feigned indifference and pretended to look at the swimsuits, but he accidentally grabbed a mannequin's chest.

Minori continued to assail him with her words. "Yeah, earlier Taiga said, 'Ryuuji's super good at household work and stuff.' She was bragging about you, like, 'Ryuuji can do a whole bunch of things I can't.' I was so surprised since it was the first time I'd heard Taiga praise anyone, let alone a boy."

"..."

"Oh dear, Takasu-kun, even if it's a mannequin, you can't grab it like that. It'll pop right off."

"T-Taiga said that? About me? What?" He was so shocked he thought his eyeballs might pop out.

It was absurd. There was no way. Taiga only ever called him a perverted dog, didn't she? There was no way she'd *praise* him.

Right—I get it. Ryuuji's eyes flashed with realization: Minori was lying. At least, she was blowing whatever Taiga had said out of proportion. She was always trying to get him to go out with Taiga, after all.

"I don't believe that," Ryuuji said.

"You don't believe me? Well, I guess that's your choice, Takasu." Minori laughed slightly and shrugged. "It's such a waste." Even after she said that, he still couldn't believe it—not even if the words were coming from his adored Minori.

It's not like anyone would believe that, right? Not when it came to Taiga. Especially not after what he'd endured over the last few tense days.

"How's this swimsuit?"

Ryuuji and Minori turned toward the voice behind them.

"Whoa!"

"Wow!"

Tee-hee. Ami tilted her head and smiled 'bashfully.' Her beauty made the desolate station seem to fade away. The milky perfection of her skin, without a stray hair or dull patch, was almost unreal.

"What do you think?" Ami asked. "It's not weird, right? If I wear a plain swimsuit like this, I won't stand out, will I? Actually, I'm a little embarrassed being in the same pool as the boys."

When she blinked slowly, she seemed to envelop her surroundings in radiant light, as though she were inlaid with fragments of stars.

"What is it with those long legs?! All ya do is stand out!"

Minori had snapped.

Ryuuji had to agree. *This is criminal, no matter how you look at it.*

Ami's eyes widened, her hair swaying as she tilted her head. She opened her eyes even wider as if in sincere wonder.

"Oh, but I chose a really plain swimsuit. That's so strange. I wonder what about it stands out? I have no idea. I wonder what it could be?"

It had been a few weeks since she had been accused of hiding her fat. Maybe it was because she had stopped stress eating, but Ami's stomach was absolutely flat and her body was perfectly toned. The swimsuit itself was dark colored and mature against her long, ivory legs and limber arms.

Even though she was slender and tall, her petite face was all eyes, alluring and charming as a fairy.

So this is a pro model...

Ryuuji and Minori were speechless.

Ami was checking herself in the mirror while saying, "That's weird. I have no idea." She was too perfect. Her legs were too long. She was too slim. Her skin was too fair. She was too beautiful.

Then, like someone waking from a dream, Minori snapped out of it and took a step toward Ami. "K-Kawashima-san! What brand is that swimsuit?! I don't think I'll look as good, but I want to look thin! I'll get something from that brand, too!"

"There were a ton of suits behind the changing rooms. Oh, do you want to get matching ones, Minori-chan?"

"Anything but that! I don't want people comparing us!" Minori rushed away with the goal of finding the swimsuit section that had the same brand as Ami's.

And then, it happened.

"Hm hmmm."

The look in Ami's eyes changed in the mirror's reflection.

Even though Ryuuji knew it was coming, he was struck by the radical change. He needed to stay composed.

Ami pivoted and put one hand on her hip, the other hand to her mouth, and leaned forward to emphasize her chest. "This is amazing, right? It's way too incredible, right? I'm way! Way! Way! Too cute! Isn't it scary? Is it okay that I'm this adorable? I'm so much more gorgeous this year than last year and even cuter today than I was yesterday! How far can I go? Can I get any more beautiful?! And, like, with this swimsuit? With this plain, ordinary swimsuit that barely cost a thousand yen?! No way! If I wore a bikini, I wonder what would happen?!"

She seemed pleased.

"Ahhh, it's scary even for me," she continued. "Come to think of it, maybe I should become a gravure pinup model? Isn't hiding this figure basically a crime? I want to see it ♥. Don't you agree, Takasu-kun?"

"Aren't you embarrassed wandering around in that getup?" Ryuuji asked. "You know we're inside a store, right?"

"Huuuh?~ Oh, Takasu-kun, leave the jokes to those eyes of yours. I'm so frickin' pretty, what's there to be embarrassed about? People who see me are so lucky. I should charge three thousand yen per person. Oh, and I mean three thousand yen per second, of course."

As Ami slowly gathered her hair up, she shed her angelic mask completely. The horribly cool, clear eyes of her true self flickered nastily. She smirked, completely aware of her beauty. She pouted her lips, teasing and mean.

"The permanent hair removal holds up!" she said.

He didn't know if she was tossing him a bone, or if it was for some other reason, but she lifted her arms in a sexy pose to show him her perfectly smooth armpits.

"Um, you know..."

"Ahhh, I'm super cute today, too~ ♥" She winked at her own reflection. Ami seemed to be in a good mood, smitten with her perfect, swimsuit-clad body.

But there was something more important to Ryuuji.

"Ummm... I-I...wonder how this looks?! I fit into it at least."

It was Minori, who poked out only her head from the changing room curtain and was calling out to Ami.

"Ohhh, which one? Let me see!"

Ami's sandals slapped as she ran over to Minori.

Ohhh, which one? Ryuuji wanted to ask, wishing he could follow, but that, of course, wasn't something he could do...was it?

Pretending to look at towels and goggles, he sidled toward them and desperately pricked his ears.

"Minori-chan, come out. If you don't look at yourself in the big mirror, you won't be able to tell if it fits."

"What?! N-n-n-no way, I-I-I-I-I-I-I-I can't!"

"You'll be in front of the whole class tomorrow anyway."

"That's completely different! Ah!!!"

"What, no way, you're super cute! It looks really good on you, and you're not fat at all, Minori-chan! You even have nice muscles around your shoulders, it looks really good!"

"Y-you think so? Really?"

"Yeah! He's already here, so why don't you have Takasu-kun look? Getting a boy's opinion is important, after all. Right, Takasu-kuuun?!"

"Hey!" Minori cried. "No, no, no! Takasu-kun, don't come! You can't look!"

Ryuuji froze for almost ten full seconds. He wouldn't look if she told him not to. He wouldn't let his interest show on his face. Though his eyes glinted with a dangerous sheen, Ryuuji tried pretending he hadn't heard. He was trying so hard to be respectable that he'd bitten through his lower lip.

Once he was sure Minori had safely returned to the changing room, he turned around.

"Huhhh," Ami said.

"Wh-what?" Ryuuji asked.

Still in her swimsuit, Ami stared at Ryuuji, intent, scrutiniz-ing, and spiteful, as if she were examining an X-ray. "So, Takasu-kun, you can't look at Minori's swimsuit? Hmmm."

"Huh?! She said not to look so I—"

"Why are you so flustered? Never mind. I'm going to put on my clothes." Taking off her high-heeled sandals, Ami sauntered barefoot through the store as though she hadn't heard him.

Somehow or other, he had been left behind, a weirdo stand-ing all alone in the swimsuit section.

The looks the other customers and the employees were giving him made him anxious. Wasn't it dangerous to have a male high school student loitering in the women's swimsuit department? As he wandered uneasily around, hoping someone would save him, he realized the person he was most familiar with had yet to materialize.

"Where's Taiga?"

There were four changing rooms, one in each corner of the square floor. One of those was open, and Minori and Ami were using the other two.

As he approached the last changing room, he saw strappy shoes in a size he recognized. *Maybe Taiga was just changing in there,* he thought.

The changing room curtain opened just ten centimeters. And, of course, Taiga's head suddenly poked out of it. She started looking around like she was searching for something. Her mouth was a straight line, and her forehead furrowed as if she was troubled and looking for help.

He thought he ought to say something, but before he could, Taiga saw him.

"Ryuuji..." she called out to him, her face unhappily contorted. She stuck a finger out past the curtain, beckoning him.

Ryuuji didn't think anything good could come of this based on the cold war they'd been waging the last few days, but if she called him, he couldn't *not* go.

"What?" he asked.

He didn't know what she would do to him later if he didn't. Probably call him a miserable dog. Maybe she'd be right.

"Just come over here," she said. "Come closer! Closer! Over here!"

As if worried someone would notice her, she gestured more urgently, her expression sour.

Ryuuji took a step, then another, toward the changing room. But as she ordered him to approach, what he was worried about was...

"There's...no way you're naked in there, right...? WHOA!"

He was attacked.

A pair of hands burst through the curtains and yanked him into the changing room in the blink of an eye. Like a Venus flytrap that had caught its prey, she closed the curtain tightly, and the changing room immediately dimmed.

Ryuuji was so surprised, he didn't make a sound, but lost his balance, hit the mirror, and fell hard on his butt.

"Ow... Tsk... What are you doing?!"

"Quiet! They'll think we're perverts!"

Ryuuji realized belatedly that he was trapped with Taiga in a space just a half-tatami-mat wide.

Taiga was at least properly clothed in her uniform (she wasn't naked after all). She plunked down on the floor beside him. "I don't know what to do anymore!" she whispered.

"Wait, wait, wait?!"

Still holding on to Ryuuji's arm, her eyes began turning red as if she were about to cry.

This was bad.

"What? What's wrong?!" Ryuuji tried to make his voice as quiet as possible. Desperately trying to somehow soothe Taiga, he looked at her face. "Don't cry! Kushieda and Kawashima will wonder what's going on!"

"B-but, but I just can't decide!"

He saw the identical black and navy swimsuits scattered on the floor around them, turned inside out as though she'd already tried them all on.

"Why're you crying about not being able to decide on a swim-suit?! Ahhh! These are still on sale, so you have to take care of them."

"I have a lot on my mind!" Taiga shook her head back and forth like she was throwing a tantrum.

Ryuuji knew if he went about this the wrong way, she'd flail and rage at him, so he automatically went into worry mode instead. "O-okay. Keep calm. First off, don't cry. Do you not like the pattern? Do you not like the color? Do you want me to bring you a different one?

Taiga shook her head more fervently. "No! I-It's the sizing that's the problem! I hate it!"

I see.

Ryuuji thought he understood: Adult swimsuits likely wouldn't work with her childish physique. "Uhhh... What about kids' sizes?"

"I'd rather die! You sound like Kawashima Ami! Ah!" she wailed in a muffled voice. She was on the verge of tears.

"Wait, shouldn't you be talking to Kushieda or Kawashima instead of me about this kind of thing?"

"If I could, I would! But they wouldn't understand. Those two have figures that work for them. It's so embarrassing that I can't talk about it! And it's none of that two-faced girl's business!"

"Look, even if you tell me that, I don't know what I can do," Ryuuji said. "Huh, what about this one?" As he began methodically putting the merchandise back on the hangers, he noticed one swimsuit that was smaller than the rest. "It's an extra small. Did you try it? Did this one not fit either?"

"I tried it. I did, but...that's... Well, it was sort of okay. But... like...o-one part of my body was..." Her voice went quieter and quieter until he couldn't hear her at all.

"Then wouldn't this one be fine?" Ryuuji asked. "I think I can fix it to fit you. Oh, this is also extra small, but it's still pretty big for you."

Out of the ten swimsuits, he found three particularly small ones. According to Taiga, those were all "sort of okay."

"Then choose one of these. What about this one? The price is reasonable, and the material is pretty thick and looks sturdy. Maybe you can also put it in the dryer?" Ryuuji checked the machine wash instructions. "I think it'll work." He handed it to Taiga, and she took it more obediently than he expected.

She looked at it intently, then between it and Ryuuji's face several times.

"Okay," she said. "You're right. This is...the best one...right...?" She sighed.

The air in the changing room was suddenly so melancholic it felt like a funeral parlor.

Taiga refused Minori and Ami's invitation to go to Pseudo-bucks (the Sudoh coffee stand and bar), and Ryuuji was hesitant to get drinks with girls by himself, so the two of them headed home together. For the first time in a long while, Taiga wasn't angry or annoyed. She just muttered, "You should have gone."

She isn't angry or annoyed. Good, I don't know why, but it seems like Taiga's mood is finally beginning to improve.

Ryuuji noticed his mistake around six thirty that evening.

"Okay, food's done," he said.

"..."

"I think the miso soup's good, and we have pudding for later."

"..."

The lump of fluff and frills sprawled beside the table wasn't making preparing dinner any easier. Without a word, Taiga poked at the greens clipped to the birdcage with her fingers. Her eyes were unfocused, and she sighed occasionally.

She didn't even seem to care that her long hair was tangled. Taiga looked legitimately depressed.

While washing the cucumbers he had pulled from the Takasu-family-recipe rice-bran, Ryuuji watched to make sure Inko-chan wasn't being stressed out again.

"Woold jyoo?" With her beak, the parakeet gently pushed the greens Taiga was fidgeting with outside of the cage. Inko-chan might have been trying to say, "Would you?"

Taiga shook her head. "I don't need any," she said quietly.

Taiga and the parakeet were having a conversation. Though Taiga was being polite to the bird, she looked like a drowned corpse sinking into a deep sea. Her body was limp, and her eyes were distant and dull. Her wrath had been replaced by sadness. It seemed like she had even abandoned her ego.

Ryuuji didn't know why she had suddenly become so despondent. Well, no, he suspected it was because of the swimsuit given the time frame, but he didn't understand why she was so distressed. She had bought the swimsuit, after all.

"T-Taiga. I tried making fried chicken in vinegar sauce today. It's the first time I've made it, but I think it went really well."

"..."

"You put mayonnaise on it. On top, here."

"..."

He couldn't lure her out of it with food. This may have been better than the cold war from the day before, but nothing could beat the banality of the current situation.

The sound of agitated footsteps broke the silence. "Ahhh, I'm late, I'm late~" cried Yasuko. "I forgot I had an interview with a girl~ I've only got ten minutes until I have to leave~"

"Huh?! What are you doing?" Ryuuji asked. "Here, hurry up and eat... Whoa! Today's getup is something!"

"You think so?~" Yasuko laughed. "Mya ha. ☆" She lifted both her hands up to the ceiling. It seemed she was trying to make the "Y" in "Yasuko."

Then again, because of her lifted leg, she might have been trying to be the Glico running man. Even her son didn't know which it was.

She really didn't look like she was in her thirties dressed like that. She was wearing a white tube top and a miniskirt that barely covered her butt. Yasuko's enormous bust stretched out her top and swayed.

They're like mounds of mochi. How do women function with those things? Ryuuji wondered, cocking his head to the side.

And then—

"Ahhh! Taiga-chan's pervy-wurvy touchy-wouchy~"

Who knew what she was thinking. As she was still rolling around on the floor, Taiga twisted around toward Yasuko, who was sitting next to her, and began groping Yasuko's mochi-mounds.

"Taiga! Don't sexually harass my mom!"

"Awww, it's fine, Ryuu-chan!" Yasuko said. "At least Taiga isn't acting scary today. It's been a long time~ Tee-hee!"

Wobble wobble wobble wobble—though Taiga continued to prod at Yasuko's breasts, her eyes were as murky as a dead fish's.

"Th-that's kind of horrifying," Ryuuji said. "So stop. Seriously. Here, look! It's your dinner! Stop touching those!"

Ryuuji briskly put the bowls and plates on the table.

"Food! Food!" Yasuko obediently picked up her chopsticks.

Still tight-lipped, Taiga righted herself into a sitting position.

"I'm digging in!" Yasuko said. "Yay, it looks good~ I love you, Ryuu-chan!~" Her chest bounced as she smiled, her face innocent and immaculately made up.

"Ahhh~"

"Ah! Hey!"

Taiga had prodded at Yasuko's breasts with the ends of her chopsticks again.

Once Yasuko hurried to her night shift, cradling her one and only precious Chanel bag, an awkward silence descended on the Takasu household.

Although Taiga ate her meal and sprawled out on the tatami

mats like always, she was staring vacantly at the corner of the ceiling. Well, her eyes were open, anyway.

Seriously, what happened to her? Is she okay? As Ryuuji finished the dishes and dried his hands, he stole a glance at her. Although he was worried, at least she wasn't aggressive like she'd been before, and she hadn't been physically hurt, so he was thinking of leaving her alone.

"Uhhh, Taiga?" he asked. "Are you prepared for swimming tomorrow? Do you have your towel and stuff? Did you put them in your bag? I'll fix the sizing of the swimsuit you bought today if you bring it over."

But he really couldn't say anything after seeing her pale face robbed of its usual fiery temper. It was like looking behind a bush and discovering the cat that always stole your side dishes had gotten sick. His chest filled with something that was maybe sympathy and maybe the urge to meddle.

"Hey," he said.

Taiga pretended not to hear him. She rolled over, turning her slender back to Ryuuji.

"The swimsuit doesn't fit you, right?" he continued. "If that's fine with you, then I don't care."

"Shuddup," she said in an incredibly small, cold voice, her back still to him. She said it like she was spitting it out. Though wounded, she was still a tiger and knew exactly how to pinpoint the most vulnerable part of his heart.

It hurt.

He had been worried about Taiga's sudden loss of spirit. And now, despite trying to be considerate and humble, despite offering to fix her swimsuit for her, despite the fact he'd done all sorts of things, she'd said, *Shuddup*? What kind of reply was that?

It wasn't as if the irritation that had been building in him all day had disappeared. Why did she have to blame him when all she had seen was Ami's teasing? She had just been pretending to cling to him, but Taiga couldn't see that. Day after day, Taiga claimed she wasn't angry and didn't care what he did but still inflicted her sour attitude on him.

Now, she went a step further and said, "You know what? You're a real loudmouth."

Fine. Like a viper, Ryuuji narrowed his eyes. He was at the end of his rope.

"Ohhh, is that right?! In that case, I really *don't care!* I'm not gonna take care of you anymore! Go swimming in something that doesn't fit you!"

"It doesn't matter because I'm skipping the swimming classes."

"Right, fine, whatever. Skip if you want! See if I care when you're held back a grade! You're so stubborn! What gives you the right to abuse me just because you saw Kawashima on top of me?! No matter who you ask, it's obvious that's what's bugging you!"

Irritated, Taiga got up, the movement as unexpected and terrifying as a wind-up doll suddenly coming to life.

Ryuuji swallowed the rest of his words.

"Why are you bringing that up now?" Taiga asked. Her eyes were bloodshot, likely because of her pent-up anger.

She bit down on her contorted lip so hard, her teeth threatened to shred it. She was as frightening as a corpse doll. This was bad. Ryuuji felt like he'd stepped on a land mine.

"Well, uh..." He stood and took a step back.

Taiga followed, her bare feet hitting the tatami mat. Her large eyes shone, wet and overflowing with murderous intent. Ryuuji could almost smell her bloodthirst.

"Hey, Ryuuji..." Her low, constricted voice licked over the back of Ryuuji's neck. "I've already told you so, so, so, so many times. I don't care about that. I'm not mad. If I looked mad, it was because you're delusional. You thought you knew what I wanted. Don't you get it? Do you really not *get that*? Hey. Hey. Hey, hey, hey, hey, hey, hey!"

Like a tank, Taiga continued moving forward slowly but surely. She jabbed her elbow again and again into Ryuuji's chest. Nonchalantly, she stepped firmly on Ryuuji's foot with her bare toes.

"Ahhh!" Now Ryuuji was trapped.

"Hey! Why don't you say something?!"

"Well, I—"

"Shuddup! Quiet! You got that?! Take my next words to heart! What happened back then *doesn't matter!* This is completely different! You got that?!"

"Well, I don't know what you're upset about this time."

"I'm going home."

Taiga fell silent. She quickly flipped her hair and began walking to the door, but Ryuuji intercepted her. He stepped between her and the door, arms waving, desperate to keep Taiga from escaping.

"Wait a sec!" he said. "It's not going to end that easily. You've just been saying whatever you want and whatever's convenient for you!"

"I'm done! Shut up! I don't care!"

He had already stepped on the land mine. How much more rage could be left to explode?

"You think you can eat a meal at somebody's house looking depressed like that and then just say you're headed home?!" he asked. "Tell me what happened!"

"Why don't you go gossip with the landlady downstairs, you rubbernecking dog!"

"Yeah, I will, but only after you tell me why you're so depressed!"

"It doesn't have to do with you!"

"Why do you hate the pool?!"

"Fine! I can't swim! I don't like it!"

"If that were the real reason, you wouldn't say it so easily!"

Taiga clicked her tongue and pivoted, her body low to the ground as she masterfully tried scurrying under Ryuuji's arm—or so he thought.

Taiga was definitely not a girl who did the expected in times like these.

"Ah?! Ow! Why is there a bean here?!" She stepped on a soybean on the tatami and fell on her butt.

"Opportunity strikes!" The moment Taiga plopped down, Ryuuji firmly stepped on her outspread skirt.

"What are you doing, you stupid dog! Let go, get off! You'll spread your canine athlete's foot all over the frills!"

"You can tell me to shut up or say whatever you want!"

Taiga struggled to stand, but Ryuuji had pinned her near her waist so she couldn't get up at all. When she made a frantic attempt to get her feet under her, the elastic on the waist stretched and fell, exposing an alarming amount of her pale side, her hip, and even a glance of her underwear.

"What?! I'm done with this!" she screamed. "Ryuuji's violating me with a bean!"

"Don't be ridiculous! This bean was left over from the home-made soy milk Yasuko drinks in the morning!"

"Ya-chan drinks this?!"

"Since when did you start calling her that?! Ahhh, you idiot!"

Taiga, working on some unknown thought process, suddenly picked up that bean, threw it, and caught it in her mouth. She had eaten it—she had eaten the trampled bean. *Crunch! Crunch! Crunch!* She chewed three times and swallowed.

"Gross! Another!" she declared.

"Of course it's gross! Uuugh, that's so disgusting! What are you doing?! You'll make yourself sick!"

"But I want to get the isoflavones!"

"Huh?"

He still had her skirt pinned as she wailed. Ryuuji looked down at Taiga's face and, at that time, was struck by a stroke of inspiration.

He recalled the time when Yasuko had declared, *"I'm drinking soy milk every day from now on. Because there's the isobonbons or something that makes your breasts bigger. I saw it on TV~ I can't have them deflate on me, so I'm thinking ahead~ I'm brilliant!"*

Then he recalled Taiga crying in the changing room because she couldn't choose a swimsuit.

"But...how do I put this...? One part of my body is..."

Isoflavones. Soybeans. Eating it off the ground. Refusing to go to swimming class. Her despondency about her swimsuit...

"T-Taiga...it can't be that...you..."

"N-no! Don't say it! Don't say anything else."

With frightened, imploring eyes, Taiga firmly wrapped her cardigan over her chest and vigorously looked up at Ryuuji. She scurried to the wall and desperately shook her head, asking him to do anything but put it into words.

But he had to say it.

If he didn't say it and confirm it was the truth, his everyday life with Taiga wouldn't be able to continue.

"Are you flat-chested?!"

"EEK—"

No one else knew the truth about the connection between the shrieks of a small tiger that resonated through the apartment building that night and the rent increase that haunted Ryuuji for years to come.

Cheeks hollow and expression as clear as if she'd just expelled a demon, Taiga said, "Wait here for a while. If you open this door, I'll kill you."

They were in the living room of the luxury condo Taiga lived in. They had walked there together from the Takasu's house, which took ten seconds on foot.

In the room that, as usual, was sensibly put together but too big for one person, Ryuuji perched himself on the edge of the sofa and waited for Taiga to return. Taiga had locked herself in her bedroom and was rummaging for something.

The glittering, modern chandelier faintly lit the cream-colored room. It was quiet. The soundproofing was probably miles above the Takasu's place, but silence still felt like the calm before the storm.

"Is that really something you need to worry about," Ryuuji muttered to himself. "Do you really need to worry about how big your chest is?"

He pulled a dishtowel out of his pocket and wiped down the low glass table while he waited.

Though it hadn't been that long since they had met in the spring, Ryuuji and Taiga's living situation had been intense. Was it possible Taiga hated being small so much that she made herself sick over it?

Just the other day, she had been withdrawn as she grumbled about her strange name and her small height. When Ryuuji found her, she was close to blowing a fuse because she liked Kitamura but couldn't do anything about it. Taiga was a strangely high-strung person to begin with, so her temper was certainly part of the problem. And now Taiga was saying she was depressed over the size of her chest, too.

She had such a pretty face, and she was loved by a friend as amazing as Minori, and she lived in a luxurious condo—he couldn't understand how she could be so unhappy. No, actually, this condo was probably one of the reasons why she was depressed. Ryuuji inhaled reflexively.

It was practically a symbol of her parent's abandonment.

Maybe her dysfunctional family was why her personality was so unsettled? He didn't want to blame everything on family issues, which seemed to be the current fad, but he couldn't rule it out.

Taiga was the outrageous Palmtop Tiger—prone to anger, dejection, and suddenly bursting into tears. Moments after abusing him, she would ask for his help. In the end, Ryuuji couldn't just not take care of Taiga when she was like that. He couldn't abandon her. No one at school could possibly understand her mental state; they just assumed she was like a carnivore loose in the fields.

I have to take this seriously, Ryuuji thought as he dusted the table legs until they sparkled. He decided to stick by the unsettled, depressed tiger.

I'm a dragon, you're a tiger, and the two are always paired together. He was also keeping the pledge he had already made. If he had to support her anyway, he would take her mental health seriously.

Right. He would say something like, *The problem isn't the size of your chest, it's that you think that's the problem.*

"Ryuuji."

"Yeah?!"

"What do you think?"

"Uhhh...uh..."

Nope. No, no, no. That is definitely the problem.

He was so taken by surprise, he fell off the sofa and received the full force of the sight before him upside down.

Taiga had slipped through the bedroom door. To validate her anxiety, she was wearing the navy swimsuit she had bought that day. Its price tag was still on it.

Her hip-length hair softly clung to her too-thin body.

Her arms and legs were pearly gray in the dim light.

Because she was so petite, he had assumed her physique was the same as a child's, but her waist was surprisingly small, and her delicate body wasn't just thin.

"What do you think of it?"

Her expression was sullen, but her beautiful face looked like

it had been carved from delicate glass. In that swimsuit, she was so beautifully molded that she could have been turned into a figure and put on display.

"You really are kind of flat," Ryuuji said.

The thick fabric easily bound Taiga's chest. He could tell it wasn't that she didn't have anything there—the slight curve from the top of her snow-white chest cast a shadow. That was most likely from her breasts, which had been flattened down. The reason for Taiga's "flatness" probably wasn't because her chest was small but because her breast tissue was too soft.

And, because she didn't have the curve that should have been between her underarm and mid-back, her swimsuit looked pitifully close to falling down with even the slightest movement. It was as if that part of her anatomy wouldn't work no matter the swimsuit's size.

"Did you try putting cups in?"

"They're in... ha ha ha, but...they cave in...ha ha." Expressionless, Taiga tried laughing to distance herself. Taking a deep breath, she threw herself onto a leather-backed chair made by a famous Scandinavian designer.

Then, Ryuuji realized something strange. "H-huh?"

He wanted to be diligent about figuring out the reason why Taiga looked flat chested, but he couldn't get himself to look at her anymore.

When he saw her exposed snow-white skin, her feminine, slender body, and her hips, which were like a glass vessel that would break even when held carefully in both hands, he was filled with dread.

He almost felt like just looking at her was violence—but he would never hurt her, he wasn't allowed to. He felt like he had to hold himself back.

"I'm flat, right?" Taiga said. "I don't have anything there. That's why I don't want to go to swimming class."

Even Taiga's quiet voice went in one ear and out the other.

If Ryuuji were honest, Ami was more beautiful when she was in the swimsuit at the station building. She had a good, perfectly-honed figure. But, in Ami's presence, he had been flustered and his thoughts had run wild. He hadn't felt this sense of dread. Maybe it was because Ami was a popular model on break and her job was to be looked at? She was beautiful and too perfect, so maybe it was because she didn't seem real? *But, but, but but—*

"Ryuuji, are you listening?"

Taiga, who was staring at him, was super real and existed right here. She was real to the point that it hurt, to the point of rawness. If he stretched his hand out, he could easily grab her. And she would be thirty-six degrees Celsius.

"A-anyway, put something on. You'll catch a cold."

Taiga nodded at Ryuuji's words and returned to her bedroom to get a bathrobe. He looked briefly at the closed door.

"Ah, ah, ah, ah, ah..."

Then he put his hands to his face and rubbed.

What was this? What could it be? Why did he have to feel so strange? And then, on top of everything, he felt so guilty his whole body quaked. He hadn't done anything, he hadn't done anything wrong at all; so what could his crime have been?

"Last year, I wasn't this worried about it," Taiga said, now in a bathrobe. "Or actually, I hadn't noticed it. I didn't notice that I didn't have a chest. We didn't have swimming in junior high, either."

Having finally recovered from his strange mood, Ryuuji nodded as he listened to her. It was Taiga's condo, but Ryuuji was the one who made tea and put out snacks.

"I went to swimming class like normal. But I found out some boy from another class sneaked a picture of me in my swimsuit and was passing it around."

"Come to think of it, there was someone doing stuff like that," Ryuuji said.

"Of course, I raided the photography club room he was using as his hideout and made it rain blood."

"And the photography club did suddenly disband."

"So, this is the picture I confiscated from them. If you look at this, I think even you'll be able to comprehend a miniscule amount of my sorrow."

He innocently took the picture she handed to him right-side down. He flipped it. "Whoa! That's terrible!"

"Ughhh..."

The Taiga in the picture had shorter hair, which she had pulled behind her head into a bun. She stood by the poolside with a sullen, bored expression.

Either the one who had been handing it out, or the owner of the picture, had drawn an arrow in sharpie pointing to her chest, and had written, "Puny boobs."

"Puny boobs... Puny! That's when I finally knew it! I realized people pitied my flat chest!"

"Well, wait a sec! That's just the opinion of whoever wrote this."

"No! Because when I look in the mirror, even I think they're pathetic. Waaah, I hate it!" Taiga wailed and put her face on the table. "I have to expose my pathetic body in front of Kitamura. What time is it? It's already past nine. We have swimming class in just twelve hours. I don't want that... I don't..."

Ryuuji's eyes were as sharp as knives. He held his tongue. He wasn't planning to attack a scantily dressed Taiga—he was thinking.

"I got it. I'll do something about it."

"Huh?" Taiga raised her face and looked at him.

Ryuuji nodded heavily. "I said I'd resize it. I have a secret plan. Take off that swimsuit and lend it to me for tonight. It'll probably be an all-nighter, but, some way or another, I'll make it so you can go in front of Kitamura with your chest held high."

"R-Ryuuji..."

Then, for the first time in nearly a week, the light came back to Taiga's wide eyes. She stared straight at him without any doubt and blinked as innocently as a child. "Really? Why would you go so far to help me?"

"Because I told you: I'm a dragon, you're a tiger. That's all."

Of course, he couldn't tell her it was out of guilt for the strange feeling he had earlier.

"You can go home and sleep."

"No, I'll wait here until it's done."

They'd gone back to the Takasu's house and had their first normal conversation in a while in the small two-bedroom apartment. Well, it wasn't exactly a *normal* conversation...

"I'll stay up with you and wait until you finish it," Taiga said. "I'm playing this game."

"Taiga...you..."

He couldn't call the conversation normal when Taiga was looking at him so kindly. Even before the incident with Ami, he hadn't heard her speak in such a calm voice.

And she was saying things like: "I was... I was being kind of stubborn and really weird this whole time... I'm... I'm sorry..."

Even if it was a bother, even if abandoning it would be easier, if you held it dear and watched it for a while, an egg would eventually hatch into a cute chick. Ryuuji felt like a mother hen, his emotions warmed and deeply moved. He was a sucker for domestic dramas, and this hit him right in the tear ducts. He felt lucky that that emotion neatly washed away the last few dregs of his sin.

In the end, Ryuuji's dedicated needlework continued past three in the morning.

"Huh? Wait? Huuuh! What's that?! Isn't that amazing?!"

"Ryuuji, you focus on that."

When he turned to look at it, he saw the words "36 chain" dancing on the TV screen for the first time in his life.

3

"**M**Y BELLY BUTTON's kinda dirty. I noticed it yesterday and dipped one of my sis's cotton swabs in oil to scrape it out, but it turned red instead. Does it look bad? Hey, Noto, does my belly button look gross?"

"No one's going to look at your belly button. More importantly, do you think my armpit hair's long? Is it too thick? It's kind of sticking out from the front even when I put my arms down, but what do you think? I only cut off my nipple hairs with scissors. Takasu, let me take a quick look at your armpit."

"Stop it. Neither of you look weird at all. And you can hide your belly button and armpits, can't you? I've been worried about this lately but...are my nipples kind of dark? If they get sunburned, do you think they could get darker?"

Aaah...

They were lined up in a row: long-haired and flippant Haruta;

Noto with his black-framed glasses and a towel wrapped around himself as he walked; and Ryuuji, the one with eyes that glinted like a beast as he eyed his swimsuit-clad companions' nipples. He wasn't imagining ripping them off—he was comparing their nipple colors to his.

They were at that age. They all had body issues.

"Agh, it looks cold..."

Before their appointment with the pool, they stood stock-still in front of the line of showers.

And, of course, the showers were left on, spouting fresh water that splattered their bare feet with a spray cold enough to give them goosebumps. They had to go in it.

"Uuuuuuggghhhhhh! It's cold!"

After only two hours of sleep, the unforgivingly cold water felt like it was piercing Ryuuji's skin. He frantically cracked his eyes to check on his friends on either side of him.

"Basically, as long as your crotch is clean, it's fine, right? Isn't this good enough?"

Haruta was trying his best to avoid the water as he opened his swimsuit waist. He let the shower stream into his swimsuit and was wailing about everything shrinking. Noto was on the other side of him.

"Eek, it's cold! Like, you know how in elementary school and stuff, there would always be some kid who would pretend to be doing a religious ritual under the shower?" He was beginning to wax nostalgic as his lips turned blue. Then, next to him...

"Clear your mind of all worldly thoughts and the shower is nothing! Nan-myo-horenn-gekyo-nan-myo!"

"Look! There's one even in high school!"

For some reason, the class representative Kitamura Yuusaku still had his glasses on as he joined his hands together like a ninja beneath the shower spray.

What an idiot, Ryuuji thought, staring from a distance at the person who was supposedly his friend.

"Oh, your glasses!"

Kitamura's glasses were knocked off by the force of the shower. The silly, austere priest fumbled after them as they washed toward the drain.

Does Taiga really like this guy?

It seemed the version of Kitamura the boys saw and the version of Kitamura the girls saw were completely different.

"Yay, this feels great!"

"Oh, Maruo! Maruo! Show us your muscles!"

"My muscles? Like this?"

Kyaaah! The girls' cheers burst out like glitter underneath the harsh blue summer sky.

"The weather's clear!"

"The water's surface is shining like waves!!!"

"It's summer!!!"

"Summer's heeeeeerrrrrre!!!"

"Only over there," Noto said.

"Yeah, it's cold here. Isn't June a little too early for the pool?" said Haruta.

The three gloomy bench sitters, Noto, Haruta, and Ryuuji, were in agreement. They watched the group of radiant girls who surrounded Kitamura from the side of the pool, letting their pale-haired shins float as they occasionally kicked and splashed. Everyone was mostly free to do what they wanted during swim classes at the school, so no one cared whether the students were swimming or sulking at the side of the pool.

At the edge of the boys' vision, the group of girls surrounding Kitamura raised their voices in even brighter laughter. "Aren't his abs amazing?!" "Yeah, they're amazing!" Apparently, they were. It may have been because he was part of a sports club, but Kitamura's upper body was amazingly taut even when seen from afar. He looked completely different than he did in his uniform— in a good way. With his glasses off, his face was handsome. Even when he squinted, unable to see, the long, tapered shape of his eyes looked really great.

"Maruo, you look better without glasses! You should try contacts!"

Holding a beach ball and floating in the pool, Kihara Maya turned her bright smile to Kitamura where he was by the poolside.

"I'm not wearing glasses today either, though," Noto said. "Occasionally, I think I'm invisible to the girls. Like, am I even here? I actually exist, right?"

"Isn't it good enough they don't avoid you because they're scared of you?"

"Jeez, you two. Don't look like you're going to a funeral."

Sitting in the middle, Haruta wrapped his arms around their shoulders. In front of the boys, directly in their line of sight was...

"Ah! You've really done it!"

"Nooo! It's freezing!"

A bursting laugh. The spattering spray. The girls' shouts of joy.

Maya, who was splashing water and laughing loudly, had her straight, long hair up in a messy bun that day. The loose hair clinging to her neck might have looked good. Her bathing suit was black. It was made to close at the back of her neck, so her back was fully exposed. Her delicate shoulder blades and the curve of her back shone like gold in the sunlight.

"Eighty-three points!" Noto said.

"Ah, that's dirty. Noto, you're already above eighty. Hmmm... eighty-five!" Haruta said.

"You two really like Kihara. I'd say seventy-seven points."

"Really? Well, kogal-style girls aren't your thing, Takasu."

"I'm just scared of them."

Ryuuji's friends agreed. From the outside, Ryuuji looked like the scariest person there, but their friendship compensated for it.

Maya's friend, Kashii Nanako, came into view. "If you stop wearing glasses, you wouldn't be Maruo-kun anymore," she said. "I think glasses suit you."

She was another striking girl in class 2-C—one of the two forward kickers at the front line. She was strolling around the poolside to stand close to Kitamura.

"Huh, Kashii, you're not getting in?" Kitamura asked.

When the revered Kitamura, who was affectionately called Maruo by the girls, addressed her, she shook her head elegantly.

"The teachers caught me slathering on sunscreen and told me not to get in the water today," she said. "Guess I got unlucky."

Her loosely curled hair draped over her shoulders in a way that made it obvious she had never intended on swimming. The moles around her mouth were as sexy as ever. Compared to Maya, her figure traced a slightly softer and plumper line, and her swimsuit, which was navy but nearly purple, had shoulder straps that were tied into ribbons.

"I want those undone! Eighty-six!" said Noto.

"I do, too! Eighty-one!" added Haruta.

"I think those are probably sewn down so they look like they're tied. But eighty-five," Ryuuji said.

The three of them nodded together and grinned. One of them had eyes more dangerous than those of a lecher.

Then it happened.

"Oh, Ami-chan's here now! No way, that's super cute! You're sooo thin!"

"Sorry, Maya-chan, I was having a bad hair day and ended up running late~"

Haruta lurched forward without hesitation.

Noto suddenly put on his glasses, which had been wrapped up in his towel.

Ryuuji leaned back, his expression doubtful.

"I'm glad, I love the pool!" Ami said. "It's my first time swimming since becoming friends with everyone! That's special, right? I was really looking forward to this!"

Ami, who had appeared at the poolside, stood slightly pigeon-toed with her innocent, angelic smile on. She waved broadly at them with both arms.

The swimsuit she bought the day before wrapped around her as if it were part of her body. Every eye in the place was glued to her.

"I'm kind of getting really emotional!"

"She's like a living goddess!"

Haruta and Noto sneakily applauded. Only Ryuuji was uninterested, remembering Ami's true nature and imagining what she must really be thinking:

Hm hmmm! I'm super cute today, too! Now, bow down and worship this angel! You have my permission, you peasants! Lick my shadow, it must be a gourmet feast to you all! Mwa ha ha ha!

Of course, Ami's exterior showed none of that.

"Ahhh, I'm itching to swim!" she said. "I haven't been able to go to the gym since I moved here! Maybe I'll give it my all and swim a lap!"

Graceful as a ballerina, she stretched her arms and legs and walked toward the diving board, the center of attention.

"Ah! Hey, Ami, you have to warm up properly first!"

She lightly waved away the warning of her childhood friend with a, "I know that, Yuusaku, you're too nosy."

"Uwaaah! She's so cool!" Haruta said.

Haruta's vocal admiration was warranted. Ami's form was magnificent as she dove, slipping into the water. When they thought she was about to resurface, she sped up. Her technique was perfect, and she obviously knew what she was doing. Ami swam twenty-five meters in one go. Then, she performed an incredibly beautiful, natural flip turn that was magnificently compact. She swam a butterfly stroke on the way back.

Even Ryuuji was captivated as he watched. Her form was amazing, and she was quick as a dolphin. Even the spray she splashed up sparkled like jewels.

"Phah! Ahhh, my eyes hurt. I should have worn goggles."

As Ami surfaced, slightly out of breath, unanimous applause rose from the class.

"Huh? What happened?"

Ami's large eyes opened wide as she tilted her head as if perplexed, though she knew very well what the applause was for. "Huh?~ Really, stop it, I'm so embarrassed~ I just used to swim every day at the gym, that's all~ You make me want to applaud all of you for being so kind~"

She clapped her hands lightly as she blushed, which, of course, earned her more praise.

"That's so cute~"

"She's so kind~"

"She's like an angel~"

"No way, seriously! I'm glad I got to be in the same class as Ami-tan! Right, Noto? Right, Takasu? Takasu, why do you look so out of it?"

"W-well..." said Ryuuji.

"The pool's really great!" said Noto.

With a broad smile, Noto began kicking and splashing. He got drops of water on his glasses. Haruta and Ryuuji joined him.

"It's really great!"

"It's just great!"

Even they had finally been swept up by summer.

There really wasn't anything more fun than swimming class and the pool.

They could see what types of figures the girls they knew had under their uniforms. The skin on their chests, their inner thighs, their butts, their underarms; everyone could equally, legally enjoy the sight during this one time of the year. The school's swimming class was mostly just fun and games, so they didn't have to worry about exams or grades or anything like that. They could also spend the PE period like this. For most of the students, this was their favorite period.

But, of course, there were girls other than Ami and Maya and Nanako.

"Hmmm. Ten, ten, fifteen, twenty," Haruta said. "That group's pretty dull. Come on, do a better job."

"Fifty-five, fifty-four. Hmmm...forty-eight," Noto said. "Why do girls who are the same level of cuteness stick together? Well, I guess that means they're all average."

Blind to their own shortcomings, they were sometimes scathing in their critique.

"Hey, why is Koigakubo here? Isn't she an English instructor?"

Following Noto's gaze, Ryuuji saw their homeroom teacher. Koigakubo Yuri (twenty-nine and single), in a tracksuit with a parasol, gloves, a hat, and sunglasses—a full-spectrum UV protection outfit. She was with a group of visiting girls, staring at the ruckus going on in the pool.

Haruta laughed slightly. "Yuri-chan's probably got her eye on that Kuro-muscle."

The one with the ridiculous nickname was the single male gym teacher (thirty-four years old, named Kuroma—Ryuuji didn't know his first name) who Haruta indicated with his chin. Kuroma was sprawled by the poolside and seemed to be devoting himself to tanning his Kuro-muscles. And it did seem like Yuri was looking at that burly, glistening back.

Ryuuji sighed. "If I say she seems desperate, that'd sound kind of pitiful."

"Of course it's pitiful," Haruta said. "According to the downlow, Yuri-chan's birthday is in September. I heard she has a goal of dating for one month, being engaged for one month, and registering her marriage in a rush right before she turns thirty! Why is she worrying about that kind of stuff? Like, it doesn't have to be Kuroma. If Yuri-chan asked me, I'd probably date her."

"Koigakubo's desperate, and Haruta's delusional. Kinky! Takasu, let's go swim a little."

"Don't say that! I'll swim, too."

Their skin was beginning to scorch, and it was a good time to cool themselves, so the three boys dropped into the pool. It had seemed cold until that point, but maybe because of their homeroom teacher's feverish gaze, or maybe because of Ryuuji's stupid friends, the temperature now seemed perfect.

"All right, let's have a showdown! We'll swim underwater over there! The loser buys the juice!"

"All right, let's do it!"

"Then we're off now!"

Then, just as Ryuuji was about to submerge…

Betraying his friends, he let out all the air he had filled his lungs with. "Phooow." He firmly grabbed the edge of the pool and didn't turn toward his friends, who had started their underwater race. His eyes opened wide, glinting with dangerous light. It wasn't that his drugs had worn off—she had arrived. She had, unfortunately, arrived.

Nobody could possibly know what was going through Ryuuji's mind.

He had actually been searching for her all this while.

She's not here, he'd been thinking the whole time.

"Oh, Takasu-kuuun! How is it?! Is the water cold?!"

Minori jogged to the pool, her smile, a perfect complement to midsummer, more dazzling than the sun.

"Minorin, don't run! My hair will come undone!" cried Taiga, who was following her. She had secured her hair into two large buns above her ears like a Chinese girl and was wearing a white parka over her swimsuit. Taiga noticed Ryuuji and gave him a slight, offhanded nod. He returned her nod and checked that the "goods" he had made overnight were functioning smoothly.

But it wasn't the time to be doing that. Minori was smiling at Ryuuji. She was sparkling and running toward him, waving her hand as if she were moving in slow motion. Her hair was in a high ponytail. Her navy swimsuit was old-school. He couldn't understand why she needed to diet—her waist was perfectly cinched, and her swimsuit held up her voluminous chest.

It may have been because she was in a sports club, but her carefree limbs were tanned. Her forearms and the skin below her knees (but above her sock lines) were baked a slight golden brown.

"Aha ha ha ha! I'll run a quick lap around the pool and get my stretching in! Just kidding!"

"Whoa!"

Minori ran in front of Ryuuji's enchanted, feverish gaze but suddenly changed direction and dashed toward the pool. *SPLASH!* Still smiling, she fell in face-first in a spray of water.

"M-Minorin!" Taiga gaped at Minori.

Splish. Minori's head emerged. "Aha ha ha ha haaa! It feels nice!" Then, immediately, she waved at Ryuuji, who was in the pool beside her. "Yo!"

She turned to Taiga. "Taiga, lend me a hand! I'm coming back out!"

"O-okay!"

"Just kidding!" Minori let go of Taiga's hand. Still posing like she was about to climb over the edge of the pool, she dove in again back-first—or rather, she fell in again. "Aha ha ha ha haaa!"

Like a submarine, she surfaced. As though she didn't mind that she'd messed up her hair or anything else, she let out a loud, heartfelt laugh. Was this really the same Minori who had been so embarrassed being in a swimsuit the day before?

As if she'd read his mind, the soaked Minori gave Ryuuji a thumbs-up.

"Yeah, Takasu-kun! I figured it out. If I get into the pool, nobody will see my belly! So, I'm gonna swim! Ciao!"

With a rowdy front crawl, she was off.

"Wh-what was that?" Dumbfounded, Ryuuji watched her, then it hit him: He'd only seen Minori in her swimsuit for two seconds. Because he had been surprised by her sudden appearance, he could barely remember those precious few moments.

"Oh no..."

"Don't make such a creepy face. You really are a perverted dog, aren't you?"

Taiga, who had been left behind, plopped herself down on the side of the pool, still in her parka.

"It's cold," she said sullenly, dipping her toes into the pool for one second.

Ryuuji aimed and squirted water at that pouting face with his hands "There!" He had developed this technique when he was in his sixth year of elementary school: It was the super high-pressure Takasu-style water gun.

"Nya!" Taiga blinked several times and rubbed her wet face with her parka sleeve. "Wh-what are you doing, you idiot?!"

"We're finally in the pool, don't look so bored."

"I'm *fine*! I hate the pool anyway!"

She smacked the water using her feet with a *flop flop flop flop!* A towering column of water assaulted Ryuuji.

"Bwah, stop it!"

"There! That's payback for what you just did!"

How was that payback when she was just relaxed and sitting at the side of the pool?

"Just watch!" Ryuuji forcefully flipped around toward Taiga and swung his arms, trying to get her with the water.

Taiga quickly turned and avoided it.

"Oh, pleh!" Kitamura, who had at some point come to stand by Taiga's back, was the one who got a face full of water. "It got up my nose! What a shock! So you two were still horsing around?!"

The apple of Taiga's eye had made an appearance, half-naked, with a body so taut the other boys were jealous. Without his glasses, he was so handsome the nickname Maruo no longer applied.

Taiga pulled her parka hood over her head, cinching it until only her nose was visible. She squirmed, embarrassed.

"T-Taiga?" Ryuuji stammered.

"Huh? What happened?" Kitamura asked. "Aisaka, that's you, right? I don't have my glasses on, so I can't really see, but you're Aisaka-sized. Why are you hiding your head? I was going to tell you your hair buns look good, like mouse ears. Are you not feeling well?"

Happy that Kitamura seemed unable to see her movements, Taiga squirmed to her heart's content.

"It's nothing, it's nothing." She repeated the words like an incantation, and then, as the cherry on top, she made a remark that she'd probably later regret, "Go away!"

"Huh?" Kitamura sounded sad. "What did I say? Why are you being so cold? Takasu, if I did something, could you point it out to me?" He furrowed his brows.

Taiga couldn't see him because of her hood.

From the pool, Ryuuji shrugged. "Beats me."

"It's fiiine! You can stop! I told you I'm fine!" Like a shark that had had its fin cut off and was struggling on a ship deck, Taiga flailed until Kitamura finally left.

"Daughhhhhhhhhhhh! I thought I was gonna die!" *SPLASH!* She dunked her red, flushed face in the pool water.

"What're you doing?" Ryuuji asked. "You finally got a chance to talk to him and you blew it. I don't want to hear you complain about it later."

"It's fiiine! Because, because, because...because I'm embarrassed!"

She scrubbed her face with water again! And again! Until her bangs were drenched.

Taiga giggled. "He said I'm good-looking, right?"

"He didn't say you were good-looking. He said your hair looked good."

"Good means good-looking. Hee hee."

"He also said he didn't have his glasses on and couldn't really see."

"He said I looked like a mouse. Mice are cute, right? Ho ho!"

Taiga lightly grasped each of her buns with her hands, one in the right and one in the left, tilted her head, and smiled like a sleepy cat. Because she had her hood on, her buns were undoing themselves. She didn't seem to notice.

Ah. Ryuuji scratched his head. Even though it was summer and they were finally in the pool, Taiga was still the same.

But, well, this is peaceful.

The water's surface glittered a vibrant blue, and the joyful voices of his friends reverberated through the air.

The weather was clear, and there was no wind.

This is good. Ryuuji watched Taiga, who was worriedly touching her bangs, and nodded. *Days like this really are the best.*

Taiga was laughing foolishly over Kitamura. Minori was somewhere else cutting through the water like an alligator and scaring Maya and the other girls who were playing with the beach ball. Kitamura was talking with Kuro-muscle about something with the attendance records in hand. Taiga had scared Haruta and Noto so they wouldn't come back. Their homeroom teacher continued to feverishly watch Kuro-muscle. Come to think of it, Ami was nowhere in sight.

Then...

"Oh my, Aisaka-san? So you're *finally here*? I thought maybe your swimsuit was so disgracefully baggy you couldn't come out in front of everyone."

There Ami was.

She wrung out her hair. She was dripping wet and smiling as if she were in a sunscreen commercial. Her voice was sickeningly sweet.

The peaceful day was about to be disrupted by a vicious tiger versus Chihuahua showdown. Ryuuji watched them unhappily.

"My swimsuit?" Taiga said. "What are you talking about? Are you talking in your sleep? Are you dreaming right now?" Her demeanor had made a complete transformation. She was composed; her gaze was cold as she smiled, as if she hadn't been anguishing a moment ago.

"Oh, that's right," she continued. "There's an idiot saying stupid things about my swimsuit. It's starting to get hot, so I guess I'll take off my parka."

Taiga stood swiftly and slipped off the parka covering her slim body.

She haughtily thrust up her chin and puffed out her chest, her delicate limbs exposed. Though she was short, she was perfectly proportioned with no excess fat, like a delicate anime figure.

The only thing hiding the ferocious tiger's naked body was a thin swimsuit.

The pool went silent.

And then, *Whoaaa*. Their classmates' voices were like a rumble in the earth.

Ami held her tongue as the class took in Taiga's ivory skin.

Like Ryuuji had until the day before, everyone must have assumed the Palmtop Tiger was built like a child with a flat chest, desperately thin and curve-less.

But behold.

"Ahhh, it'd be such a pain to get a sunburn because I'd turn red."

She lidded her eyes, her eyelashes dropping shadows on her cheeks and hiding any anguish she might have felt. Taiga twisted so they could see her waist and straight, limber back. Her long legs were crossed. She was slender but had proper feminine curves. And those boobs.

A smirk that might have put him in jail slid over Ryuuji's face.

They were too perfect.

They weren't huge, but they definitely weren't small. They naturally swelled from her swimsuit, like magnificent domes; one on the left and another on the right. When Taiga casually and triumphantly turned her body, they jiggled softly. Ryuuji called them "faux breast pads." He had sewn the finest of masterpieces overnight.

He had taken pads from some of Yasuko's old clothes, layering them as he cut them. He piled them on top each other to create a subtle gradation and, stitch by stitch, had carefully and skill-fully sewn them together with flawless needlework that would put a pro to shame. There wasn't a single lose thread, and they were held in place by invisible snaps. When Taiga tried it on that morning in the early dawn, she had been so deeply moved by the inhuman craftsmanship that she blushed. She swore she would absolutely take it with her to her wedding.

"What? You've got a regular figure, that's no fun. Well, it's still all wrong since it's miniaturized anyway," Ami muttered. Her true maliciousness slipped onto her face for just a moment.

"You're stupid," Taiga said, then, turning her back to Ami, gave Ryuuji a small fist pump. "We did it."

Ryuuji fist pumped back

The boys who had seen the photo from the year before began whispering.

"It's amazing what one year will do."

"I can testify her boobs grew well."

"I'm definitely on Team Tiger."

Everyone had been thoroughly deceived.

Taiga was in a rare good mood. She smiled and sat by the pool once again with her feet in the water.

"Ryuuji, show me how you did that thing earlier," she said. "That squirt thing you just did. I'm going to do it to Minorin."

Ryuuji brought his hands together and showed her how to make the water gun. "First you put your hands completely to-gether, right? Then, you just put them in the water and..."

"Like this?"

Taiga obediently put her hands together and stooped forward to put them into the pool's water. *Fooled you!* Ryuuji thought as he aimed at her face from close quarters.

"Like this."

Squirt. He covered her in water.

"Ufuh! Why you!"

She wiped her wet face with the back of her hand and glared at Ryuuji.

"Fine," she said. "I'll do it back at you. Don't move. Stay right there."

Taiga tried to mimic what Ryuuji had done and filled her hands with water. She forcefully squeezed her hands to make a jet.

And splashed her own face.

"Upuh!"

She was a terrible klutz, and sometimes stupid, besides. Without thinking, Ryuuji burst into laughter, and gaining audacity, he attacked her again.

"Like this, like this! Why can't you do it?! It's like this!"

"No! Wait! Upuh! Ryuuji! You can't...habluh!"

Taiga tried desperately to avoid his attacks, but she couldn't open her eyes or stand up. She frantically covered her face with her hands. For the first time in his life, he had an advantage over Taiga.

"There, it's like this!"

His pride didn't last long.

"Hey! Don't bully Taiga!"

"Bwah!"

BAM! He was assaulted by a heavy blow that was like nothing he'd ever felt before. Water shot down his nose and throat like bullets. It took him several more seconds to realize it was being shot from Minori's hands, and from quite far away, at that.

"Mwa ha ha ha! How's that? How's the power of the Kushieda family's secret water gun that's been passed down over generations?!"

"H-how did you just do that?!" Ryuuji asked. "That hurt a lot!"

"I won't tell anyone who bullies Taiga!"

Minori flashed a peace sign and swam skillfully to the center of the pool where the water was the deepest. This was par for the course for the mad dog from Kanto. Well, no, not really. But anything that required a strong arm or that had to do with sports really was her forte.

"Minorin, thanks for saving me!" Taiga smiled at her savior.

Her eyes sparkled, but Minori took one glance at Taiga and grinned.

"The fake boob squadron."

Leaving them with those words, she disappeared under water. Like an alligator skimming beneath the surface, she cast a dubious shadow.

"Sh-she knew..."

"Of course Minorin would know."

The two stood still by the poolside, shivering. They felt

the sudden instinct to clasp each other's hands and stick close together.

Then, on the other side of the pool, *BAM!* A violent splash of water rose up. They looked over in surprise.

"Ha ha ha ha! How's that?! Being all popular by yourself!"

"We question the disparity of the social classes!"

The high-pitched laughter came from Noto and Haruta, who were poolside. Finally, Kitamura's face emerged from the water.

"Y-you guys!" He coughed. "Argh, damn it, I'm going to get you back!"

With two sidestrokes, Kitamura, who Taiga had driven away, got out of the pool and caught Noto, who was running away. Class representative or not, he threw Noto from up high with a suplex.

"S-s-s-stop, my glasses, my glasses! *Waaaaaahhhhhh!*"

"This is the summer arrival DRRRRRRRRROP!"

He forcefully twisted himself, and, together, they dove backward into the pool. A column of water spurted up.

Someone else nabbed Haruta. His arms and legs flailed as he was forcefully lifted off his feet.

"Go, my cradle from hell!"

SPLASH! He was thrown into the pool.

"Now it's a party!"

"I'll throw you right in!"

The pool erupted in screams. People were pushed and fell in. Anyone who tried to crawl out again was kicked back in.

"Stop stop sto... Nooo!" Nanako, who had been taking a graceful afternoon nap, was hurled in at the other side.

A battle royale between the boys and girls had begun.

"Wah, wait! This is dangerous!" Ryuuji tried to get out of the pool but was splashed by someone flailing past him. He stepped onto the ledge.

"Prey detected!"

"Let's go, softball alliance!"

"Huh? Wah, ahhh!"

On the right was Minori. On the left, Kitamura. The moment he noticed them, they grabbed his arms and threw him backward into the pool.

Ryuuji struggled to get his face above the churning water.

"Ah, those guys! Cough, cough, cough!"

The softball alliance hurried to catch their next victim.

"What?! No way?! There's no way?!" Maya shrieked.

In front of Ryuuji, Taiga rolled around laughing. "Ahhh! Did you not want to be thrown in?! At least Minorin touched you."

She happily looked down on Ryuuji. As expected of the Palmtop Tiger, there wasn't a person in the class capable of throwing her into the water.

"D-damn it! Would you rather I throw you?" Ryuuji asked.

Should I? he thought.

And that was when it happened.

"Just. Found. You ♥. Here's a brat who still hasn't been pushed in yet ♥."

A sinister voice came from behind Taiga. It could only be one person: Kawashima Ami.

"Y-you!" Taiga had let her guard down and couldn't find her feet fast enough.

"Heave ho!" Ami grabbed her by the armpits and picked her right up. "It's just a game, just a game ♥. You can't get mad for reeeaaal! Hah!"

"GYAAAaaaaaaaaaaaaaH!

SPLOOSH! Ami threw Taiga in. With a massive splash, Taiga sank into the water.

"Ha ha ha ha! Look at what she's doing!"

"I-If you have time to say that, shouldn't you be trying to run away?!"

"I want to see that insolent tiger's face as she cries!"

Ami was practically dancing, but Taiga didn't surface. *Plip, plip, plip.* Only bubbles came floating up, and, eventually, even those disappeared.

"H-huh?"

Time seemed to stretch, then it came to Ryuuji. *Hadn't Taiga said something? It was, it was, uhhh... I asked her, "Why do you hate the pool?!" And Taiga said, "I can't swim! I don't like it!" Or something.*

Uhhh, which basically means...

"She can't swim?! She's drowning?!"

"Huh? Seriously?"

Ami's face turned blue. In the same moment, Ryuuji quickly

took a breath, went under, and kicked the wall. Three frantic strokes and his hand reached Taiga, who was balled up in the water. He surged upward with her in one push.

"Puhah! Hey, are you okay?!" he asked. "Hey, hey, hey, hey, hey?!"

"I-I-I-It's not the time for thawghhhhhh!"

Taiga floundered and struggled trying to get out of Ryuuji's arms. She pushed his chin away and the two of them sank into the water. She inhaled water through her nose, still struggling for dear life. Ryuuji somehow managed to get her head above the water.

"I'm in trouble aghhhhhhhh! Blaughhhhhh! What should I dwooo?!" she cried.

"Wh-what are you aughhhghw?!"

Still choking on water, her reddened eyes were desperately searching for something. Instead of grabbing Ryuuji, she clutched at her own chest as if she was trying to hide it.

"Y-you don't mean—aughhhwgh?!"

"It came out aughghghg! J-just one side bleeeghh!"

She could only mean one thing.

"Eek?!"

Several meters away, it floated—the faux breast pad. Before anyone else found it, Ryuuji made a desperate grab and successfully retrieved the pad while still holding Taiga with one arm.

"It can't be true, right?! Why didn't you say you couldn't swim?!"

"Gyaaa, no, don't come near me baghaghaghgh!"

It seemed that to Ami, Taiga and Ryuuji's struggling only looked like drowning. With splendid form, Ami dove in and was heading their way to rescue them. This was bad; if she saw one plump breast and the other flat as the horizon, who knew what she would say. It was now or never!

"GYAAA?!"

Ryuuji sank into the water with Taiga. He worked like lightning. Taiga struggled and burbled. With that hand—with his hand, he opened her swimsuit at her chest.

There! He stuck his hand into the warmth inside her suit and stuck the pad back to its original position. He had to do it. He might have touched something. He might have, but that couldn't be helped.

In that moment, in the water, he only knew Taiga had been trying to shout something, but only bubbles came from the tiger's wide-open mouth.

"Huh, what? What happened?!"

"Ami-chan pushed the Palmtop Tiger into the pool, right? And then..."

"Eek, isn't that *bad?*~"

Everyone in the class whispered and prodded each other with their elbows, but the incident was anything but trivial.

"I really didn't know you couldn't swim!" Ami said. "I told you I was sorry."

"An apology isn't enough."

With Ami now in front of her, all Taiga could do was roar. She had her head on her desk, her eyes glinting behind the wet ropes of her hair.

She was right. A "sorry" wasn't going to cut it. Ryuuji was practically frozen as he watched them.

Humiliated—that was the word Taiga had used after being pulled up to the poolside after *that*. Of course, she didn't mean being thrown into the pool so much as what Ryuuji had done. He thought he had been doing the right thing at the time, but maybe he had gone too far. He'd touched something with the back of his hand, and on the other side of the bubbles, too, he felt he had seen something flat.

"Because you did something as stupid as that, I was..." Taiga said.

"You were what?" Ami asked. "Did something happen?"

"Anyway, just apologize! Apologize, apologize, apologize!"

Taiga shook the desk she was leaning against so it clattered. The display of anger might have seemed like it lacked force for the Palmtop Tiger, but no one would have guessed the real reason behind it: that someone had (maybe) seen her breasts and she was humiliated.

Except Ryuuji, of course.

"Seriously, what are you saying you want me to do?" Ami said. "I just apologized a bunch of times."

With her angelic mask still on, Ami faced Taiga, but she was clearly getting frustrated. The smile on her lips was brimming faintly with poison.

"But to think, Aisaka-san, that you'd sink like a stone. I feel kind of sorry for you. How sad. I wonder if you've been really ashamed of it all this time? Maybe you've been left out of after school activities because you can't swim?" Beneath the sympathy, Ami's voice was adorned with sarcasm.

The students in the class, who had missed that sarcasm, agreed with sweet voices. "Right, so that's it."

Completely aware of the surrounding eyes, Ami began adding insult to injury.

"And it's summer," she said. "So you can't go swimming in the ocean or pool, right? No way, that's the worst. Oh, and also, if you can't go, Aisaka-san, does that mean your good pal Takasu-kun can't either? Nooo waaay, that's so terrible! Takasu-kun, *we* can go swimming if you want ♥."

Ryuuji didn't know what logic Ami had used to get here, but she seemed to believe toying with him was the most effective way to bother Taiga. Except Ryuuji was the one most bothered by it all.

"Huh. Why is Ami-chan inviting Takasu-kun out?"

"Why is it always Takasu?!"

As his classmates watched this scene develop, their eyes suddenly and noticeably changed.

No, wait a second. Ryuuji didn't want to be involved.

"Right!" Ami said. "So, Takasu-kun, my family has a villa! Do you want to go to the villa with me?"

"Huh?"

Ami passed by Taiga and stepped toward Ryuuji's side.

"Yeah, let's do that!" Ami said. "It's decided! That's fine, right?" Her Chihuahua eyes glistening, she tilted her head to the side slightly.

The classroom got noisier.

"Why Takasu?"

"Why a villa?"

"What are you doing, Ami-chan?!"

"Wait a sec!" Ryuuji said. "Why are we suddenly talking about summer? Weren't you supposed to be apologizing to Taiga?!"

"Huh? Was I?" The sham angel cocked her head and smiled, as if to say, *I totally forgot.*

"Ahhh, this is stupid! That's it! You can go wherever you please, you lecher!" Taiga made a resolute noise as she stood. She quickly walked through the gathered crowd like Moses parting the Red Sea.

Ami pouted as though slightly disappointed, but she pursued and attacked. "Let's go, let's go for sure, Takasu-kun! I'm sure it'll be fun; we can spend the whole summer together!"

"Look, cut it out," he said.

"Huh, is that not good enough? Then... Right, it'd be fine if Yuusaku came, too, right?"

Plunk.

Taiga's footsteps stopped.

She turned on her heel and once again strode through the crowd.

"Whoa?!"

Silently, and with the strength of a vice, she grabbed Ryuuji's wrist, which Ami had been holding.

"Oh my~"

"What?"

She turned him around and pushed Ryuuji behind her. Ami's eyes narrowed in as if she had found something entertaining. Although the class was in the middle of its break, it now quieted like it was a ship ready to sink. The only sound was the din of the neighboring class. Of course this would happen; to the bystanders, it looked like the Palmtop Tiger had pulled Takasu away from Ami by force, so the fickle spectators were stunned.

However, Ryuuji understood; he understood well. The thing that had made Taiga stop wasn't Ryuuji at all. It was the words, "If Yuusaku came, too."

"What's wrong, Aisaka-san?" Ami asked.

"I won't forgive you for being so selfish," Taiga said.

"Isn't that different from what you were saying earlier? Didn't you say he could go and do what he wanted?"

"It's different when it's the whole summer break. Ryuuji has to prepare my food and do all kinds of other things. So I can't let him go."

"Whaaat? Are you saying, 'Ryuuji is mine'? That's ridiculous."

"Who said that? Maybe you should go to the doctor? Or would you rather I probe those clogged ears of yours, instead?"

Ami looked down at her, her lips twitching.

Taiga looked up and arrogantly pushed out her chest.

Ryuuji, as well as everyone out of their field of vision, was waiting for the imminent explosion.

Taiga made the first move. She took a step forward without hesitation, and a smile that could only be described as bewitching appeared on her pale face. As though telling a secret, Taiga stood on her tiptoes and whispered to Ami, "If you keep being selfish like this, I'll leak the one hundred impressions in succession video... Oh, or was it one hundred fifty?"

In an instant, a shadow as dark as black blood loomed over Ami's face. However, she couldn't allow herself to shed her angelic mask. *SMI...LE.* Somehow, she managed to beam at Taiga and leaned forward to whisper back.

"If you do that, I'll slap you with a publicity rights lawsuit for illegally using my likeness. Even the Palmtop Tiger isn't above the law, right?"

"Ha...ha ha ha..."

"Aha ha..."

"Oh ho ho ho ho ho ho!"

"Aha ha ha ha ha ha ha!"

The whole class watched as blue veins pulsed on both girls' temples. Just when it seemed like one of those veins would burst—

"Stop right now! You'll only hurt your fists." Minori, risking her very life, jumped between the two and firmly grabbed Taiga's fist.

"M-Minorin?!"

"Now, now! Back away from each other! Separate! Separate!"

There! Pushing on Taiga and Ami's chests, Minori put distance between them and went into sermon mode. She belted out, "You two, cut that ooout! Taiga, Kawashima-san! I won't tell you to force yourselves into becoming closer, but you two are *waaay* too hostile! It's intolerable!"

"But, but, Minori-chan," Ami said. "Do you know what Aisaka-san did—"

"It's this dumb Chihuahua's fault! If she hadn't transferred, if she had never existed—"

"Ahhh, seriously!" Minori exclaimed. "Be quiet! Look, Taiga, don't grab her by the collar! You can't resort to hand-to-hand combat! I understand you want to nurture your friendships through your fists, but you don't have to fight. You can settle this through regular old sports instead!"

"Huuuh?!"

The only one who raised her voice was Taiga. The spectators, including Ryuuji, tilted their heads, speechless. Unable to keep up with Minori's fantastical imagination, they furrowed their brows.

Unexpectedly, Ami was humming in consideration, her face composed. "Oh, that might be fun ♥."

She skillfully lavished her dazzling smile on the class.

"Um, just so you all know, I really want to get along with

Aisaka-san!" she said. "I'm so jealous of her having fun with Takasu-kun that sometimes I say things even Takasu-kun misunderstands! But I want to eventually become friends with Aisaka-san! Look, I'm not always good with words, and I'm a little clumsy, so I'm not doing the best job of it, but I mean it!"

With this, she skillfully sewed together the seams the earlier dispute had begun to fray dangerously.

"Of course, Ami-chan wouldn't actually set her sights on Takasu for real," the class began to whisper. Ami grinned; Ryuuji recognized that expression.

The only one who refused to consent this was Taiga.

"Why?! How?! What is this? This isn't a joke! There's such a thing as being too stupid. What do you mean you want me to compete in sports with this dumb *Chihuahua*?! I'm not going to become a laughing stock. It would be an embarrassment for generations to come. Why do I have to do something like that?! And Minorin, why aren't you on my side in the first place?!"

"You idiot!" Minori chopped at the top of Taiga's head.

"Ow."

"Taiga, this is for your sake! You can do this stuff while you're a student, but this won't hold up when you're an adult! Are you going to suddenly attack your coworkers or other people when you don't like them?! Listen, if you don't do this, I'll also go to Kawashima-san's villa and we'll deepen our friendship over the summer! Amiiin! Kiss, kiss!"

"No way, Minori-chan, that's too much!"

Minori clung to Ami, kissing her white cheek.

"Being a girl must be nice," one of the boys muttered.

"Argh!" Taiga stomped her feet in frustration. "Fine! I got it! If you're going that far, Minorin, I'll do it! But, if I win, I'm starting a fan club for her video impressions!"

"Then if I win, Takasu-kun is going to spend the whole summer at my family's villa with me ♥. And then you'll be by yourself the *whooole* summer." Ami's final, venomous words were too low to reach the ears of the rubberneckers.

"Then let's go! Ba-da-da-da-da-da-da-da-da-da-da-da!"

Rousing the class with a drum roll that didn't seem like it could have possibly come from a human mouth, Minori closed her eyes, thrusting her hand into a plastic convenience store bag and stirring the contents. Inside were two pieces of paper folded and cut to the same size. On one, Taiga had written a method of competition, and Ami had written an idea on the other.

"Ta-da!"

Drum roll complete, Minori grabbed one of the paper slips.

Ryuuji and the rest of the class hovered behind Taiga and Ami as Minori, standing at the teacher's podium, opened the paper. Minori finally cleared her throat, and the class pricked their ears.

"Hyoo! Shyoo! Jyoo!"

Pop. A gigantic question mark seemed to appear over class 2-C. What were those foreign-sounding words supposed to mean?

"Oh, that was an imitation of the late David Jones," Minori said. "He was a foreigner who was famous for presenting the Pan American trophy at sumo championships on the closing day. And on top of that, we look alike."

At Kitamura's exclamation of, "Why do you know that?" another question mark added itself above the class.

"Just kidding!" said Minori. "Now, the time for games is over. I'm going to announce it! Uhhh, the sporting event showdown will be..."

Minori grinned at Ami, then faced Taiga and frowned.

"Kawashima-san's proposal, the 'twenty-five-meter freestyle one-game match!'"

The class applauded.

Ami lavished her surroundings with curtseys. "Yay, lucky me!" she exclaimed.

Taiga's mouth contorted. Beside her, Ryuuji's eyes glinted. Even though the drawing had been fair, a swimming competition was just a cruel method to inflict on Taiga, who couldn't swim.

"This is pretty much a done deal," their classmates muttered.

The day of the match was the last swimming class of the semester. Incidentally, Taiga's proposal had apparently been Vale Tudo.

"THIS CLASS IS EXCELLENT. Most of the first years were drowsy after they were done swimming."

The teacher looked down from the top of the platform at the students of class 2-C with a broad grin. Everyone's eyes were wide open; they didn't seem like they'd just come from swimming at all. The teacher didn't notice the strange tension running through the silence like an electric current.

Of course, Ryuuji's eyes were wide open, and he wasn't following along with the textbook or anything else at all. His composure had been stolen, his focus blurred, and all he could think of was what had happened earlier.

How had it become such a big deal? Why had he gotten wrapped up in this?

Ah. He bit the end of his pencil.

"Hm?"

Someone threw a folded note over his head. It hit the back of the chair of the person in front of him and dropped with a plop onto Ryuuji's desk. From behind him, he heard a small groan of, "Ah, oh no..." They had probably tried to skip Ryuuji by throwing the note to the seat in front of him but blundered. Ryuuji, who was a kind soul, poked at the back of the person in front of him and tried to pass it to them. Then, he noticed the writing on the front of the note.

"Can I take a look, too?"

It said, "Pass to everyone in class 2-C!" *I'm part of the class, too, aren't I?* He propped up his textbook to hide the note and opened up the B5-size sheet of paper. His sanpaku eyes lit up.

"The First Takasu Cup Opening Competition! Ami-tan vs. The Palmtop Tiger, 500 yen each! Note: Pass around to everyone except Ami-tan, Tiger, Takasu, and Judge Kushieda."

"What is this?"

His softly glinting eyes swiveled around the class.

"Who was the klutz?!" someone murmured.

"Ahhh! That idiot!"

Everyone avoided Ryuuji's gaze and awkwardly looked away. *How terrible!*

This was just too much. Ryuuji bit his thin lips; they had made him into the butt of a joke.

Several people had also left comments expressing their participation on the loose-leaf note. There was a line drawn down the middle; on the left, someone had written "Ami-tan" and on the right they had written "Tiger." Apparently, each person was supposed to write their name in the column under who they thought would win.

So far, everyone had bet on Ami. Taiga's column was stark white.

On top of that, there were several comments scribbled on the note:

"Is this actually worth betting over?"

"If it's a swimming match, Ami's it for sure. ★ Tiger will sink."

"But if it were a fight, it'd be Tiger."

"Tiger's odds of winning are zero, right?! She's bound to lose!"

"Takasu-kun suddenly became popular, right? Why?"

"That's just because he's the pawn in Ami-tan and Tiger's bid for political power!"

"Ami-tan's not actually hanging out with him for real."

"Yeah, you're right. In the end, Ami-chan will win, and they probably won't even go to the villa or anything. That'll be the end of it."

"Tiger and Takasu are serious. But Ami's a shoo-in."

"Are you stupid?"

"No, Ami-tama is my waifu."

"Only in your dreams."

"Ami-chan's mine."

"I'm super hungry -> Is lunch here yet ->"

"I want girls to fight over me, but how do I do that?"

"Ami's mine, so sorry you @arl."

"Did you mean to write '@all?'"

"Aren't you in trouble if you can't even write 'all?' @Haruta"

"Did you like, bribe your way into this school? @Haruta"

Haruta are you...? No, this wasn't the time for that.

"What is this?" Ryuuji muttered. "They're just writing whatever they want."

This was awful. Ryuuji's eyes, sullen like his father's, grew bad-tempered. He didn't like scaring people for no reason, but he hated being the butt of something like this as much as he disliked being underestimated.

Just look at the comments the girls had left:

"Despite his face, Takasu-kun is actually really indecisive, that's why he can be used like this (lol)"

"Yeah, I agree. Takasu = pushover (lol)"

"He seems like he'd shut up and go along with anything (lol)"

"It seems like he's really been supporting Taiga-chi (lol)"

They were horrible. Absolutely horrible. He hadn't realized the girls thought he was so pitiful. They must have been joking (lol), but it gouged Ryuuji's heart.

"Damn it," he whispered. "I'm not just pitiful."

Just watch. Ryuuji took out a wide marker, letting it squeak as he wrote his own name in large letters in Taiga's column. He would bet six shares. That was three thousand yen—a whole three thousand.

It was unlikely anyone knew, but a dragon and tiger came as a set. On top of that, Ryuuji was a pretty good swimmer. They still had time until the showdown. Taiga could begin her intense training now. If anything, Taiga had potential; she could improve. She could take on Ami.

"If that happens, I'll get the whole pot," he growled in a low voice, intimidating them even further. Maybe Taiga was rubbing off on him. Ryuuji skillfully refolded the paper into an airplane, turned, and aimed at a diagonal to his back. He sent it flying in a straight line.

"Hey, Taiga?"

"Hm? What is this?"

Eep! Someone shrieked quietly. Of course, Aisaka Taiga, also known as the Palmtop Tiger, quickly grabbed the paper airplane that whizzed through the air. She opened the note slowly with her small, pale hands and muttered, "Huuuh..."

And that was it.

But that one word was cold. Her tongue, redder than blood, licked her fiercely smiling lips, which were ominously contorted into the savage smile of an animal. The color rose on her cheeks, and her white throat quivered in excitement.

"So then, someone please come to the front and work on this problem," the teacher said. "Oh, how rare. Well then, Aisaka."

Taiga stood, her eyes as predatory as a wild beast's, glimmering as if not a scrap of reason were left in them. She looked ferociously at each of her classmates.

"A-Aisaka?" said the teacher. "You don't need to march around inside the classroom. Ah, well, um, I guess you can march, but just solve the problem, okay?"

Instead of heading to the teacher's podium, Taiga walked along the lines of desks as though examining them like a two-ton tiger.

The entire class felt the intense pressure of seeing the blood-thirsty tiger stalk them. Here and there, shaking voices begged for their lives. "Eek," "Sorr..." Only when she passed by Ryuuji did she grin knowingly to confirm her bond with her comrade. The next moment, she tripped on the foot of someone's desk, but as she was falling, Ryuuji grabbed her by the waist of her skirt and her grin came back to life. As she tried to get onto the podium, she tripped again, grin still in place. She was definitely a klutz.

Then Ami, noticing the strange atmosphere even though she didn't know the circumstances, said, "Huh? What happened? Why is she so angry?" She blinked her eyes and tilted her head quizzically.

Then, just one person, just Minori, who sat on the hallway side seat, remained silent.

"Zzz...zzz..."

If you looked really, really closely, her eyelids were closed, but she had drawn eyes on them with sharpie and white out.

"Taiga, I'm gonna give you all of my support, okay?" Ryuuji said. "Don't you go and lose."

"Of course I won't. I'll make that Chihuahua girl look like a beat-up old rag in front of the whole class."

While flipping through a magazine that read, "Aim to be the

swim speed king!" on the cover, Taiga glared at Ryuuji, who was still holding cooking chopsticks.

"And of course you'd help me," she said. "If I lose to the Chihuahua, you know what'll happen to you, right?"

"Yeah, I know. I'd be locked up in Kawashima's villa for the summer, right? That's no joke. Who's going to do the laundry, clean the bath, cook, make payments, and do everything else? Look, help out a bit. Mix the vinegar miso."

Ryuuji handed Taiga a glass bowl containing the seasoning and a spoon before busying himself with wiping the table with a dishtowel.

"What are you putting it on?" Taiga asked.

"Udo root and wakame seaweed."

"Bleh. I don't like that much."

"It's good for you, so eat it. It'll make your boobs grow."

"You lying, stupid uggo."

"U...ug...uggo..."

Though she easily wounded Ryuuji, Taiga also began mixing and helping him. Like a child, she sat on the ground, pouting. "I think you should already know this, but—"

"Ahhh, yes, yes." Fed up, Ryuuji busily moved to stand and spoke over Taiga. "I got that loud and clear. You're going to say you don't care where I go or who I go with anyway, right? I know that. What you don't like is that Kitamura is going, too."

"No. Of course there's Kitamura-kun, but I actually don't want to let you go. Not to that girl's villa."

"Huh..."

Taiga's cheeks swelled up with a peevish expression as she mixed the vinegar miso.

Ryuuji looked at her profile. *Huh,* a small doubt formed in his mind. *Maybe that was...? Maybe, just as Ami said, Taiga thought of me as...*

"What would you do for food?" he asked. "If you're willing to come here three times a day from the villa, it'd be a different story."

"Oh, right. Sure, sure, I get it."

"Self-absorbed," he muttered.

"Ryuuujiiiiii?" She may have heard him. Putting the vinegar miso down with a clack, she thrust the miso-covered spoon at Ryuuji's nose. Taiga spoke slowly, as if he were a child. "Do you have any idea what you are? You're a dog. My dog. Now, say that the purpose of your life is to do as I say. Say that for the sixteen years up until you served me, you were good as dead, you male mutt!"

"Huh?! I'd never say that!"

"You say it if I tell you to say it, you say it."

Her eyes were like black voids. Taiga smiled. "You saw my breasts, didn't you?" she said. "You touched it, didn't you? How embarrassing. What a mistake. Whenever I think about it, I feel like my heart is going to squeeze out of my nose. *You* did that. Even if you offered up the remainder of your life, it wouldn't be enough. I'm the one who gets anything you've got to spare. Got that?"

Ryuuji was tongue-tied. What could he possibly say to that?

"Y-you saw my chest, too, didn't you?!" he finally managed. "Isn't it the same?! And when I saw it, it was in the water and I was all flustered, and I had no idea what was going on either."

"Haaah?! *Your* chest?! Are you talking about those pitch-black, trash raisins?!"

"Trash raisins?!"

Ryuuji's legs buckled. Her abuse was far too innovative. This was possibly the worst thing she'd ever said to him.

Taiga made a face as if she wanted to spit at him and then went back to her work mixing the vinegar miso.

"Wah!" She put too much force into mixing and the spoon flew out of her hands. It smacked into Ryuuji's temple as he hung his head.

"Ow! You...devil klutz!" The thick vinegar miso ran down Ryuuji's sorrowful cheek.

"Oh, deary dear, is dinner not done yet?~"

Finishing her preparations for her night shift, Yasuko came into the living room.

As Ryuuji rubbed away the vinegar miso, he said, "W-wait a sec, it's done." He retreated to the kitchen like a bashful bride.

As Ryuuji prepared the soup, a scene unfolded behind him.

"Ahhh~ Taiga-chaaan, you're so great for dressing the vinegar miso~ You're such a good girl for helping~"

"Y-you think?"

"I love udo root~" Her childish face prettily made up as usual,

Yasuko smiled with not a lick of maliciousness. If anything, she looked strangely happy as she took the position opposite of Taiga.

"Um, you know, I think I'd be okay showing this to you, Taiga-chan," Yasuko said.

"Huh? What is it?"

Ryuuji, who had poured the miso soup and loaded sides into bowls, was bringing them to the table. Yasuko had turned her back to her son, and was facing Taiga, so he was unaware of what was happening.

"Here you go! Taiga-chan, because you kind of seemed like you wanted to see them~"

His mother pulled her clothes right up past her breasts.

"Huh?"

Luckily for her son, who had dropped the bowls, only saw her white back. Taiga, who was sitting with her legs folded under her, opened her eyes wide and collapsed straight onto the floor.

Miii, he heard Taiga shriek faintly and pitifully. She sounded like an abandoned kitten. Maybe she was terrified of giant breasts.

The two of them didn't have time to be shocked by giant breasts or anything else.

The next day was their second swimming class of the year. It was hard to say if the slightly cloudy weather was ideal for the pool.

"There. We're doing it, Taiga."

"Here I go, Ryuuji."

Taiga and Ryuuji came to the poolside. Their eyes flashed blue-white, feverish and bloodthirsty. Or maybe it was just determination. They had their arms folded over their outthrust chests (though one was fake) and looked strong and imposing. The atmosphere around them suddenly changed. This wasn't a friendly, bustling pool, this was the beginnings of a serious showdown. Their guts and their pride, their entire summer, were on the line.

First, Ryuuji went into the pool, and then Taiga followed. People drew back as if the two had spread poison in their wake. No one talked to them, but they could hear the surrounding whispers and feel the numerous gazes that feigned nonchalance.

I get it, Ryuuji thought as he squinted one of his eyes. They were wondering how he would get Taiga, who couldn't even swim, to a point where she would be able to face Ami on an equal level. He turned his back to them.

"Let's start practicing," he said.

"Right, let's start."

He looked Taiga in the eyes as she nodded in vehement agreement. Let them say what they wanted. Using her physical strength, Taiga could easily get to a point where she could swim twenty-five meters.

"Okay, Taiga, let's start by just kicking the wall and floating."

"Ryuuji?"

"Yeah?"

"If I'm going to kick the wall, that means I have to let go of it, right?"

"That's right."

Taiga firmly gripped the pool's edge and looked quite earnestly into Ryuuji's face. The rippling water reflected blue light on her fair cheek.

"If I let go, I'll drown."

"..."

"And my feet can't touch the bottom."

Maybe they needed a few more fundamentals first. So she couldn't reach the bottom with her feet... *Hmmm*. He tapped his forehead, reconsidering his plan for a few seconds.

"Okay," Ryuuji said. "Let's start with dunking your face in. Put your face in the water. You can do that, right?"

Taiga laughed loudly. "I'm not an idiot! Of course I can do something like that. Look."

Oh, good, that's a relief. Ryuuji breathed in. "T-Taiga? Th-that's...?"

Taiga really did put her face in the water. She stretched her arms all the way out, and still holding the pool's edge, gradually sank in to just under her nose. Her large eyes looked around, and she fluttered her lashes cutely.

"Bwah! See? I did it, right?"

Hmph! She pushed out her padded chest.

Ryuuji clapped a hand to his forehead and took another few seconds to think of how to explain it to her.

"Uhhh...you dunk your head basically...like this."

Ryuuji grabbed the edge of the pool in the same way she had and properly put his face into the water. He counted out three precise seconds.

"Bweh... Right? It's different, right, from what you were doing? Hey, watch me!"

He accidentally hit Taiga's elbow as she was looking away.

"That hurt!" she cried.

"Were you watching?! Can you do what I just did?!"

"What?! Ah! Yeah?"

Although her spirits were high, Taiga's gaze wandered nervously, and she didn't meet Ryuuji's eyes at all.

Uh. A sinking feeling filled Ryuuji's chest. "Ah! So you can't do it," he said. "You can't dunk your head in."

"What?!" Taiga shamelessly turned away. She tried to whistle but wasn't able to make a noise. The terrible feeling became reality. It wasn't just a matter of whether or not she could swim; it seemed he had to start this one off with getting familiar with the water.

Hand already pressed to his forehead, he temporarily lost focus, unable to go into deep thought. Ryuuji bopped Taiga on the head to raise her spirits. She told him not to be so chummy about touching her and brushed him off.

"A-anyway, for today, you're going to just master dunking your head in the water," he said. "Unless you can do that, we can't move forward."

Though he didn't emphasize how important the basics were

as he spoke to her, they could hear the peanut gallery's whispers and gossip from beyond them.

"Hey, they're starting out with dunking her head."

"Isn't that way too easy?"

"That's something you do in the first year of elementary school, right?"

"Shouldn't she be able to do that already?"

Her pride seemed to have been wounded. Taiga's brow rapidly wrinkled, and the color of blood rushed to her cheeks.

Ryuuji tried turning and stopping the originators of the gossip from saying anything more, but it seemed he was too late.

"I-I can dunk my head under the water, so I'm not going to do that," Taiga pouted, her small nostrils flaring. Face still red, she added vehemently, "That's too easy, so I'm skipping it."

"A-are you sure that's okay?!"

"It's fine!"

Then, foolishly, she let go of the pool's edge and grabbed Ryuuji's arm. To keep her face from touching the water, she desperately elongated her body and floated, thrashing, her legs fluttering.

"Pull me!" she said. "If I just get my body used to how it feels to swim, it'll be fine!"

"Right! Is that right?"

"It's fine, do it!" she shouted like she was nipping at him.

Going backward, Ryuuji reluctantly pulled Taiga forward.

"Upuh! Upuh!"

Half of Taiga's face was in the water and she continued to desperately kick with her eyes still mostly closed. But Ryuuji was a little skeptical—*Does this actually count as practice?* Taiga, gripping him, wasn't floating. He was fully supporting both of her arms. If he didn't, her fluttering legs would sink further and further into the water until she wouldn't even be splashing.

"Upuh...mwha ha ha ha!" Taiga said. "It's going great! I can do it, I can do it, I can do it! Swimming. Is. So. Easy!"

To Taiga, it may have seemed like she was swimming. Though her expression was desperate, her spirits were incredibly high. She began laughing painfully as she raised her chin.

Then, Ryuuji suddenly remembered the time he learned how to ride a bike. When he had been in his first year of elementary school, he had taken off his training wheels for the first time. He couldn't find his balance at all and kept falling over. At that point, Yasuko had said, "I'll run with you and support you, Ryuu-chan, so just focus on peddling as hard as you can." She grabbed his bike from behind. When he pedaled, with Yasuko supporting his bike, he somehow went forward without the bike falling over. Feeling brave, he kept going faster and went forward just fine.

At some point, he suddenly realized Yasuko hadn't been behind him. He had been riding the bike all by himself. Yasuko had tripped and fallen when she began running, several meters back. She had been sticking out of a hedge with her two legs poking straight up just like Sukekiyo from *The Inugami Family* movie.

That's it, I'll do a Sukekiyo, Ryuuji thought. He would let the strength leave his hands and, in the end, he would let go of Taiga. "Huh?! I'm swimming?!" she would say, and he'd reply with, "You did it, Taiga!" *Like that. Okay, just like that.*

"Gwah cough."

"Wahhh!"

He had only slackened the strength in his hands for a moment. Taiga simply sank into the water.

"A-are you okay?!"

Taiga coughed. "Wh-what just happened? Where am I? Who am I? Who are you..."

Even her memories had been robbed from her. After a moment of panic and gasping, she cried, "You let go, didn't you?! You traitor!"

Splash! She slapped her hand on the water and splashed Ryuuji's cheek. Oh, that was good, her memories had returned and...

"Huh?! You're floating!"

"What? Huh? No way?!" Both of Taiga's hands were completely free. They were near the center of the pool where her legs wouldn't have touched the bottom, and Taiga's face was above the water.

"Uwah, I did it! I can swim!"

"You've already as good as won!"

Without thinking, the two of them tried to high five.

Of course, that wasn't what happened.

Blub blub blub blub. From behind Taiga, Minori emerged like Poseidon rising from the deep. One of her arms was wrapped around Taiga's torso.

"Takasu-kun," Minori said, "did you drop this normal Taiga in the water? Or, was it this golden Taiga you dropped?"

Minori had been supporting Taiga from within the water.

"I-It's this Taiga."

"That's right. This Taiga, who would sink as well..."

After pushing Taiga to Ryuuji, Minori once again sank into the water with a *blub blub blub*. She swayed as she swam, and Ryuuji wondered where she was going.

"Wh-what?!"

"I'm unbiased," Minori said. "Because I helped Taiga, I also have to help Amin..."

"Minori-chan, what's wrong?! You look like Poseidon! No, that tickles!"

Minori had grabbed Ami, who had been playing beach ball with Maya and the others, from behind.

Ryuuji felt like she was somehow off base.

"As expected of Minorin. She's the paragon of a fair judge and sportswoman," Taiga said. And if Taiga said it, she probably was.

Ryuuji looked at the dazzling, wet skin of Poseidon and vigorously nodded in reply.

Then, for the time being, he firmly grasped Taiga's arm and walked through the pool to get back to the edge.

"Oh dear, this is really bad."

"There's no way she'll win in that shape."

"Tiger didn't have the sense to know how to swim in the first place."

"You can't compare her to a mermaid like Ami-tan."

The two were once again surrounded by exasperated whispers. Taiga tensely bit down on her lip.

"I-I'm frustrated!"

"Owowowowow!"

Her nails pierced Ryuuji's shoulder.

"They're just saying anything they want!" she exclaimed. "They're saying I can't do it at all, that I don't have the sense to... Uuuh... I feel like giving up!"

"Don't pay attention to them!" Ryuuji said.

"I know, but I'm frustrated! I'm embarrassed! I don't want this anymore, I don't want anyone to see me like this!"

"Damn it. They're all betting on Kawashima. They're trying to embarrass us and make it so we can't practice."

Ryuuji looked around, beginning to think of all his classmates, who should have been familiar to him, as enemies. Then, something even worse happened.

"Oh, how are you, Aisaka? How are you feeling?! Make sure to work hard with Takasu and give it your all!" It was Kitamura, yelling cheerfully at them from the side of the pool.

Taiga groaned and made an indescribably strange face. She couldn't even reply to him. The harder Taiga worked with Ryuuji, the more Kitamura would misunderstand her relationship with him. From the outside, it could only look like Taiga was after Ryuuji too.

Ryuuji, unable to do anything, took in a breath and made

his decision. "Okay. Let's not practice in the school's pool. We'll practice a ton somewhere else and surprise them."

"There's a heated pool on that side of the station, isn't there?" Taiga asked.

"Right, we'll use that."

And then, as if right on schedule, a single drop of rain hit the water. Another cold drop hit the tip of Taiga's white nose.

Unanimously, the class said, "It's cold!" "Was that rain?" and rushed to get out of the pool...

...which ended swimming class.

"Right, to start, Matsumoto Seichou is chosen as an Olympic flame runner. But suddenly, a strange shadow appears! Hah, it's you, Dazai Osamu! Oh nooo! He's stealing the flame! Like I'll let you! Seichou gathers his gumption and hits Dazai! Dazai nimbly throws himself into a jump to avoid him, and then, BWASH! Wounded wings emerge from his back."

"What is this? A literary battle?"

"Isn't it obvious?! It's the title sequence for that dumb Chihuahua's imitation DVD fan club. She'll have to perform it at the opening ceremony when I win."

"Seichou or Dazai, which is she supposed to do?"

"Both. One person with two roles—she has enough skill to do that."

"D-does she now...?"

"I helped her blossom."

Taiga, who was strangely excited, swayed her umbrella up and down happily as they made their way down the sidewalk in the night rain. Though he grew tired of it as he followed her, Ryuuji was in a good mood, too. Even though they'd just swum at school, they had gone to the heated pool in the outskirts of the city after dinner. He'd been able to dry their swimsuits with Taiga's strong dryer.

After the sun went down, it had begun to pour. When Taiga swayed her lavender umbrella, the spray of rain pelted Ryuuji. He skillfully avoided it with his own umbrella.

"First is definitely dunking your head," he said. "Then, we'll float you with a kickboard and practice kicking." Ryuuji recalled what he'd learned in swim class when he was younger. He was serious about Taiga's practice schedule.

They still had days to practice, so from then on, they would go to the heated pool every day and...

"Huh?"

At Taiga's voice, he looked up and fell silent.

"Huh? Wait, you've got to be kidding me!"

The gate that should have led to the heated pool was firmly closed with an iron padlock. They had come in such high spirits— how could it be closed? Then Ryuuji looked toward the building and was even more shocked.

There stood two bulldozers, motionless now because of the rain or the time of day. They had stopped in the middle of demolishing the buildings on either side of the pool into rubble.

"Huuuh?!" Taiga exclaimed.

He noticed a plate lying at Taiga's feet and picked it up as she raised her voice. There were words written in sharpie on it.

"Thank you for your long patronage," he read in amazement. "'We have decided to close our heated pool. The year after next, it is to become a library.' A *library*?"

"We don't need a *library*!" Taiga's voice shook.

Ryuuji imagined his plan crashing down and adding to the rubble before his eyes.

Taiga can't even dunk her head underwater.

Taiga can't practice at the school's pool.

Taiga can't swim

Taiga is going to lose.

Then Ryuuji would be taken to Ami's villa for the summer. Which meant...

"Oh ho ho ♥. Won't it be fun? It'll definitely be fun. Now, have some fruit ♥."

Leaning on him, her white body boldly straddling Ryuuji's legs as he sat on a sofa in the resort, a swimsuit-clad Ami offered him fruit.

"Here, say 'ahhh' ♥. It's ripe pineapple I got from my villa ♥. Have a bite."

Wait, no, don't come that close to me. *But she was in a swimsuit, and he was hesitant to touch her skin to push her off. Ryuuji had no choice but to open his mouth. And then...*

"Takasu-kun, you have to let me play, too! Taiga's not here, and

I'm bored! Hey, let's play softball? Takasu-kun, what's your favorite position? First base? Or second? Or maybe third?"

Of course, Minori was wearing a swimsuit and had a glove on one hand. She stood in the doorway, beckoning Ryuuji. It was paradise. Out of instinct and desire, he was about to wander that way and go toward her, but...

"Nooo, Takasu-kun, let's eat pineapple."

"No, no, Takasu-kun, come play second base with me."

"Come have tropical fruits with me."

"Do a bullet liner with me."

No, no, no, no! I have people waiting for me. People in a gloomy, two-bedroom apartment where the sun doesn't shine. What did I do about their food? Oh no, I didn't even set the rice cooker. They must be hungry. *Somehow untangling himself from Ami and Minori's arms, Ryuuji began running. He sprinted to the second floor of the rental and opened the entryway door, but it was already too late.*

On the floor were three corpses. A parakeet, Taiga, and Yasuko. Yasuko had written "She starves by the seashore" on the tatami mat: Her final words.

Wait, what is this?!

"Hey. That's gross."

"Huh?"

"Your face!" Taiga cried. "You've been grinning and tearing up, and it's gross!"

Standing before the demolished main gate of the heated pool,

Taiga's yelling brought him back to reality. Right, he couldn't do that. No matter what, they needed to win.

But.

"Ahhh, what should we do?!" said Taiga. "We really can't practice anywhere except the school's pool!!"

"That's all we can do now," Ryuuji replied. "We'll need to be serious with everyone looking at us."

"I can't! Kitamura-kun will be watching."

Ryuuji didn't know what to say to that.

The pouring rain continued for a full two weeks.

Naturally, all their swimming classes were cancelled. Taiga was still completely unable to swim and couldn't practice. That she had to practice at the school's pool wasn't even a concern.

"The rain hasn't stopped."

"If it keeps up like this, will the Takasu-cup be canceled because of the rain?"

Even though it was afternoon, it was dark outside. The classroom was bright with fluorescent lighting. They should have been at swimming class right now but had settled into boring self-study instead.

In whispers around them, there were voices raising concern about the arena Taiga and Ami would compete in.

"I can't concentrate."

"I'm worried."

Taiga raised her gaze from her image training; she had been looking down at an athletic magazine with a feature on swimming. Ryuuji was pretty much taking on the role of a coach.

"If it comes to this," he said from his seat in front of her, "you just have to rely on the strength of your mind in the match." He thumbed through a back issue of the same magazine in front of Taiga, who was in a sullenly bad mood.

"It's not like I'll learn how to swim by reading this," she said.

"It's better than twiddling your thumbs. And you're also practicing flutter kicking every day at home."

The flutter kicking practice involved lining up sitting cushions on the tatami, Taiga getting on her stomach, and moving her feet earnestly as if she were kicking. "That's it, that's the spirit! Do it stronger! Faster! Wow, they say there's a hamburger steak place in Asakusa people line up for. Whoa, that looks good," he'd said.

"Why are you watching TV?!" she had shouted.

And then, "Owowowowow!" When her kicks hit his back, he verified firsthand they hurt a lot.

"That's not real practice," Taiga said.

"Aren't you practicing in the tub, too?"

"I am. Well, right, that might be helping the results along."

She grinned as if she had self-confidence. Incidentally, that practice only consisted of her filling the bathtub with water, going underwater, opening her eyes, and holding her breath.

"Now I can open my eyes without panicking, too," she said.

"Whoa, that's amazing!"

"Hee hee hee, I can hold my breath. For three whole seconds."

"You've as good as won!"

Yay, yay. The fellow kindred spirits forcibly psyched themselves up and tried to high five, but their hands slipped past each other and missed.

"Ahhh, how useless," said Taiga. "I want to actually practice in a pool. Why did the heated pool close down?"

"I know..."

Coming back to their senses, they looked up at the ceiling, exhausted. In the distance, someone whispered in a small voice, "They've already definitely lost, right," and even though they heard it, Taiga pouted; she couldn't even yell.

Then, a bundle of paper dropped onto Ryuuji's upturned face.

"Hey."

"Uh!" Ryuuji exclaimed. "What? Oh, it's you."

Kitamura smiled broadly at him.

BAM! Taiga flipped over in her chair.

"What, of course it's me," Kitamura said. "Now, how are you feeling? Your swimming match with Ami is coming up, isn't it?"

"It doesn't matter," Ryuuji said. "We can't practice like this. Right?"

Taiga blushed faintly and nodded. Trembling slightly, she righted herself in her seat. She tried to fix the position of her desk and was swallowed up by an athletic magazine avalanche. "Ahhh."

"You wouldn't with this weather," Kitamura said. "I don't know if you can use those, but it's a gift from me."

"By those you mean...these?"

Ryuuji looked at the papers that had been dropped on his face: They were admission tickets for a public pool.

"My mom sells insurance," Kitamura said. "She hands these out complimentarily, and she had leftovers. There are two of them. Use them. I actually bet on Aisaka."

"Huh." Taiga's eyes went wide, and her voice went soft. Surprised, she looked up at Kitamura.

"Earlier when I saw the betting sheet, I saw you were so full of confidence when you bet on Aisaka, Takasu," Kitamura continued, "so I was like, yeah, I'll do that, too. After that, a lot of other people switched over to Aisaka. You're to blame, Takasu." Pushing up his glasses, Kitamura laughed heartily deep in his throat.

Taiga, flustered, cleared her throat several times and sputtered, "Y-you...bet on me? You think I might win?"

"Yeah."

Buwah! Like a person who had an allergic reaction, Taiga's face became an even more brilliant red.

"Aisaka, you're the type who'd suddenly develop super strength in a crisis. At the very, very end, you seem like you'd turn everything on its head. If I were to compare you to a superhero, you'd be Kinnikuman. Not the second generation, though."

Was that supposed to be a compliment? Ryuuji tilted his head.

"Ah... The prince... The leading role..."

Taiga lowered her bright red face and her cheeks loosened into a grin.

What, she's happy?

"Exactly like that," Kitamura said. "But Ami, she's the type who's bad in the heat of the moment. No one knows which way the match will go. At least, that's what I think."

"Don't you think these could be split like this?" Ryuuji turned and held out one pool ticket to Taiga and the other to Kitamura.

As he did that, Taiga's eyes went round. She didn't wait for Kitamura to react.

"Daaah!" she exclaimed in a strange voice. She forcefully seized Ryuuji's arm and snatched the ticket he was holding out to Kitamura. She clutched it to her chest, and with a face so red it seemed as if it could burst into flames, looked up at Ryuuji.

Seeing that, Kitamura said, "Well, in that case, give it your all when you practice. It'd be nice if the rain stopped." He laughed, grinned broadly without even the slightest indication he felt bad about what happened, put up one hand, then left.

Ryuuji looked down at Taiga. She contorted her face as if she were about to cry. She averted her eyes.

"Aaah. You idiot." Without thinking, he gave her a fake punch with his fist on her soft, full, and hot cheek. Taiga didn't complain. She stayed silent, her eyes averted, his fist still on her cheek.

Sighing, he took the pool ticket from her small hand.

"If you keep them, you'll lose them anyway. This is for the next weekend. Hopefully the weather clears up. I'm thirsty so I'm buying juice. You want anything?"

Taiga just shook her head.

"Oh."

"Hey."

It kind of felt like déjà vu.

Two people stood in front of the vending machines when they were prohibited from being used.

"Takasu-kun, are you skipping?~"

"Look who's talking."

Crouched along the wall, Ami was drinking milk tea by herself. "Over here," she said after Ryuuji bought his iced coffee. She pressed him to sit next to her.

"Why are you by yourself in a place like this? You're such a dark person."

"Look who's talking."

In the end, they were birds of a feather, crouched side by side along the gloom of the wall. "Upsy daisy," he accidentally said, and Ami let out a laugh.

"Seriously, are you sleepy or something?" she asked.

"Of course I'm tired. Because of a certain person, I'm tired."

"Huh? Are you saying it's my fault?"

"Of course I am. Seriously, whenever you go around doing strange things, I'm the one who pays the price."

"*Strange?*~ I have no idea what you mean."

"You know what? You can do that for however long you like, until your face spasms."

Ami's expression broke free as she laughed. She threw off her pure, good girl mask, and her miraculously beautiful face clouded with a veil of spite and cool wickedness.

"I've got to tip my hat to you," he said.

Realizing she hadn't brought anyone with her and was stuck in this place by herself even though it was self-study time, Ryuuji lightly toasted his can against Ami's.

Her clear, amber eyes blinked as if she were surprised. "Huuuh?" Then they immediately narrowed, as if he'd made a joke. "What a rare thing for you to do today, Takasu-kun," she said. "You usually don't approach me. What's wrong? Oh, did the Palmtop Tiger bully you or something?"

"That's enough. That's normal. Do you know just how insistent Taiga's been about blaming me since seeing you with me?"

She laughed like a dove. "That's cute. The jealous tiger."

"It's not cute, and she's not jealous," he said. "She just gets mad that you're provoking her because she doesn't like you. She would have been angry in the same way even if the one you were with was Kushieda instead of me."

"Of course she wouldn't be. Takasu-kun, are you stupid? Do you really think if that *child* saw me chumming it up with Minori-chan in the same way she'd actually treat Minori like she treats you?"

"Don't call me stupid. That's—you're... It's *that*, right? You're both girls, and they're close friends so..."

"Ah, sure, sure, right," Ami said. "You're saying that's not jealousy. Ha ha, it's like you've been talking with her about it. 'You got jealous, didn't you?' 'This isn't jealousy.' You repeat what she says. This is *fuuun*."

Ami lightly tossed her empty can and got an amazing hole in one into the trash can. She didn't spill a single drop, didn't drop the can, and didn't miss. He hadn't needed to deploy the pocket tissues he used to combat klutziness.

"It's not *fuuun*," he said. "Stop provoking Taiga. It's making trouble for me, more than anything. And anyway, what's with the villa? You didn't actually plan on inviting me from the start, so what are you planning to do if you win? If you're planning on pretending nothing happened, Taiga won't let me go out of spite."

Ryuuji walked over to throw away his empty can.

"I don't intend to pretend like nothing happened."

At her unexpected voice, he automatically turned back to Ami.

Ami was still sitting along the wall and smiling as she looked at Ryuuji—her angel act was on. "I plan to win for real," she said. "I'm going to win and spend my summer with you, Takasu-kun. Embarrassing Aisaka Taiga is fun, but more than that, I'm really, actually thinking about my prize. What's with that face? Are you surprised?"

Ryuuji didn't know what to say; he couldn't tell if Ami's words were part of one of her bad jokes or not.

Ami, still grinning broadly, pointed at herself and Ryuuji with her thin fingertips. "I think it'll be fun, though. Because, see—we get along pretty well."

"W-we don't!"

"Aha, you're mad!"

"Listen here! Seriously, stop teasing people. Look, if you're done with your tea, go back to the classroom."

"I'm going to stay here. Why don't you go back, Takasu-kun?'

"I will but not because you told me to."

Ami frivolously waved her hand at Ryuuji with a, "Then bye." Even though she didn't have anything to drink, she stayed where she was, between the vending machines.

She really may have been an extremely dark person.

"The match is tomorrow. It came before we even realized it."

"..."

"The weather's kind of so-so. At least it's not raining."

"..."

"According to the forecast, tomorrow's supposed to be cloudy."

"Pwah! Ryuuji, did you see that just now?! Hey, hey, were you watching?!"

It would be difficult in his position to say he hadn't because he'd been watching the weather instead, so Ryuuji just nodded at her.

"Hee hee! That was pretty amazing, right?! I definitely just put my face in the water for ten whole seconds!" Taiga proudly thrust out her faux breast pads as she held the edge of the kiddie pool. She'd been dunking her head the entire time.

"Ahhh, yeah, your face was in the water, it really was," he said from the edge of the pool.

"Gah! It's a scary guy!"

"No, Ah-chan, you can't go near him!"

He was scaring the nearby women with her kids for no reason other than his looks. This wasn't even a kiddie pool, it was an infant pool. The water only came up to Ryuuji's knees.

"Oh. Hey, Ryuuji, don't I look like I'm swimming?" Taiga let go of the side of the pool and put her hands on the bottom and pretended to be an alligator, walking toward him.

"Wapuh!" Her hands slipped and she bubbled as she sank. She flailed, splashing until she finally resurfaced, gasping and choking.

"Oh dear! Ah-chan, no!"

Little Ah-chan dribbled water over Taiga's already sopping head with an elephant watering can.

"Oh no, I'm sorry for her behavior! Ah-chan!"

"Ahhh."

Ah-chan made her exit, held by her young mother.

Taiga, with an unspeakably strange expression, got up, splashing as she walked back to Ryuuji.

"Even I was helpless against that pure evil." In an extremely rare moment, the Palmtop Tiger proclaimed her defeat.

"In any case, high schoolers aren't supposed to be in the kiddie pool."

"Was that the source of Ah-chan's wrath?"

The day the rain finally stopped, they used Kitamura's public pool admission tickets.

It was a Sunday. The public pool was twenty minutes away by bus. Ryuuji and Taiga eagerly came all this way, but the clouds hadn't let up, and the sky was a dull silver. The temperature was still low, and the water was cold. Because of that, there weren't many customers, and no joyous voices reverberating around the four pools.

"Taiga, let's go to that big pool over there," Ryuuji said. "They could have built a water slide at least."

"Or a wave pool. There's one that barely flows. Wah, they're stupid, aren't they?"

Leaving behind small, wet footprints on the ground, Taiga laughed at the junior high student pretending to sit zazen cross-legged style like in a religious ritual in the "waterfall pool." He was acting as if he were under an actual waterfall. Ryuuji should have told her that Kitamura had done it, too, but he noticed an abandoned, free-to-rent swim ring that had been conveniently left on the ground before them.

"Here."

"Geh! No way! What is this?!"

He slipped the swim ring over Taiga from above. "You've got to. If you don't want to drown, hold onto that. Anyway, your feet don't touch the bottom. See, let's go to the flowing pool."

"Geeeh... it's ugly..."

The circle-shaped pool seemed kind of like it was struggling because of its slow flow. Ryuuji jumped in feet first, while Taiga timidly tried not to get her float caught as they got in.

"Uwah, wah!" Taiga cried. "My feet actually can't touch the bottom here."

"As long as you have your tube, you're fine. When you need to get out, I'll pull you up."

Ryuuji held onto Taiga's inner tube as she bobbed down the stream.

"Beginning to learn the crawl now is probably impossible," he said. "We'll just have to use an inner tube or a kickboard tomorrow."

"No way! Ahhh, that's so uncool! Why has it come to this?!"

"We can't do anything else, right? If you say, 'I'm not doing it because I couldn't learn how to swim,' that's exactly what Kawashima is aiming for. It's not a front crawl match in the first place, either. It's actually 'freestyle,' so a kickboard is probably fine."

"Freestyle, right. I wonder how *free* I can make it..."

"Look, stop smiling like you're planning something evil. Try flutter kicking a little like that. There's a current, so it should make it easier for you."

"Ugh..."

Ryuuji let go, gave the inner tube a small push, and tried to keep up with her with a breaststroke.

"Like this?" Taiga asked.

Splash splash splash splash! Columns of water rose into the air. Taiga's kicks, with the advantage of buoyancy, were impressive. Even though there was a current, her speed was outrageous. He couldn't keep up with her bursts of speed and had to switch from breaststroke to sidestroke just to follow her.

"W-wait a sec!"

The columns of water subsided and Taiga bobbed along in her inner tube, turning with the stream as it changed directions. She looked at Ryuuji quizzically as he caught up.

"Huh? I'm actually fast at swimming? It's obviously because it's a flowing pool."

"N-no, you're pretty fast. I'm also being pushed forward. Uwah, wai... I'm out of breath..."

"You think?" Taiga said. "I wonder. Then this time, I'll give it my all and you give it your all following me."

Splash splash splash! Once again, she began her flutter kicks at full blast, building speed. Normally, people with an inner tube couldn't go that fast.

"No way!" Ryuuji already couldn't keep up with a sidestroke and finally gave it his all with a front crawl. He had thought, until that day, that he was a pretty good swimmer. Someone in an inner tube shouldn't have been able to outpace him.

"U-unbelievable!"

He fell farther and farther behind Taiga's wake. The current should have made him faster, but he couldn't keep up with her at all.

Then, the splashing subsided, and Taiga stopped swimming, turning to Ryuuji as if she were bored. "You really are a lazy dog. Come to think of it, maybe I'm just really amazing? Maybe I could win like this."

"Don't get...cocky! You've got a...stream...pushing you!"

Ryuuji was completely out of breath. When he finally caught up to Taiga, he held on to her inner tube.

"No! Don't pant on me! You pervert!"

"I'm out of breath...haaa... Can't help it...haaa... It hurts..."

For a while, they drifted with the stream until he caught his breath again.

"Ahhh," Ryuuji said. "I really pushed myself swimming for the first time in a while."

As Taiga was trying to say *I see,* a yawn escaped from her open mouth. "Hwaaah..." A tear that had collected in the corner of her eye ran into the rest of the water. Ryuuji, also feeling hazy and relaxed, watched it in a stupor.

He felt strangely calm as they bobbed and drifted. It might have been because of the sound of the water, or being gently jostled around, but the two of them fell silent, bodies going with the flow.

"It kind of...feels like I could sleep right here..."

"No, no, we came here to practice, and the competition is to-morrow... Ugh, hwaaah..."

Led along by Taiga, Ryuuji yawned, too. An old man floated past, laid out still on a mat, leisurely bobbing along. An infant who looked like his grandchild rode in a round duck inner tube next to his grandfather.

Not a single person in this pool was moving forward using their own propulsive strength. They had all abandoned themselves to the current, completely, totally relaxed.

"Ahhh... This pool we came to is kind of peaceful..."

"I feel super sleepy..."

"Me, too..."

That would be the case. Because of the weather, they had been on standby watching the forecast since seven in the morning and had finally decided to leave the house at eight.

Then after that, they hadn't been able to remember whether or not they had given Inko-chan her food. Her expression had been ugly when she woke up. Yasuko had woken up grumbling with a hangover. Taiga had forgotten her hair tie at her house, and by the time they were done fussing and made it to the bus, it was nine. It was ten by the time they changed and made it into the pool.

Ryuuji felt like they had used their physical strength just getting to this spot.

"I wonder how the weather will hold up tomorrow?"

"I bet the pool will close because of rain."

Nngaaah. They both made lazy faces. Still holding on to the inner tube, they looked up at the gloomy sky. Then, as if even looking up had become bothersome, Taiga put her cheek on the inner tube like a sleepy cat.

"After doing this, I kind of...feel like...I want that to happen..." She sounded lethargic. It wasn't like he didn't understand how she felt.

"Don't say that. Kitamura bet on you. Aren't you happy? Say that."

He was trying to light a fire under Taiga using the only fuel guaranteed to work. He waited for the flames of love to start burning in her eyes, but...

"Nnngh..."

"What was what? What do you mean 'nnngh?'"

With her cheek still smooshed against the inner tube, she gazed blearily at the pool. The water on her long eyelashes glittered as it spilled onto her slender wrists.

Ryuuji pursed his thin lips without realizing what he was doing. "We came all this way, and Kitamura is cheering you on. I don't think that's a good attitude."

She didn't reply. The strands of her hair drifted along with the water, and she closed her eyes. She actually seemed like she was beginning to not care how the match would go.

Ryuuji, somehow still sullen, recalled Ami's words: *Sorry, but I actually plan to win for real. I'm planning on winning and spending my summer with you, Takasu-kun.*

As he bobbed and swayed alongside Taiga, Ryuuji considered something for the first time: Taiga may lose. She may already be losing in spirit. Other than the handicap of her being unable to swim, she also couldn't give it her all for Ryuuji in front of

Kitamura. Taiga herself probably wanted to win, but she was also falling into a lethargic trap.

If Taiga was in the same state the next day and lost, he would...

"Uh. I think I felt a drop just now?"

"No way."

As Taiga raised her face, another cold raindrop fell in front of her nose.

It was almost afternoon. They ate yakisoba from a stand for lunch while they waited for the good weather to return.

"It kind of looks like everyone's giving up and going home," Taiga said, pausing as she twirled her yakisoba.

They were under a parasol, which made for a slightly chilly rain umbrella, and still in their swimsuits.

"People do what people do," said Ryuuji. "Once the rain stops, let's go to a pool that doesn't flow this time."

"Yeah... But your lips are blue."

"You've got blue aonori seasoning all over you."

Taiga didn't seem worried by the aonori around her mouth at all. She furrowed her brow as she stretched out her hand, watching the passing shower outside the parasol. Her frown deepened.

"It's raining really hard for some reason," Taiga said.

"Has it really started coming down?"

"It's getting colder, too." Taiga showed him the goosebumps prickling her white arm. The wind chilled their bare skin without mercy.

"It wouldn't be good to catch a cold," Ryuuji said. "Guess we just have to go home after we finish eating."

At that suggestion, Taiga, who had been listless, became attentive. "We're going home?" Her expression was strangely innocent and slightly peeved. She looked at Ryuuji with some dissatisfaction.

"You've got goosebumps, haven't you? And my lips are blue. Are you okay?"

"That's true, but... But I haven't practiced at all yet. We just floated around earlier."

She stuffed her cheeks with yakisoba, adding a stubborn sounding, "Damn it!" Though she'd been hesitating earlier, she seemed to have changed direction now that the weather had worsened and didn't want to go home.

"You don't want to go home?" Ryuuji asked. "It's gotten colder, but do you still want to practice? I think it would be better if you did."

"Yeah. I'm still going to practice. It's cold. I'll get distracted. I've gotten distracted and there are a lot of other things happening, but I'm definitely going to try harder."

She was a moody person. *Oh right,* Ryuuji thought, tilting his head. Love had fueled her earlier. Maybe it had finally begun circulating through her body.

"Right," Ryuuji said. "Kitamura went out of his way to give us these tickets. That's Kitamura cheering you on. It'd be terrible to let them go to waste."

"It's not like that! It's not like that at all. The reason why I'm saying I'm going to try, the reason why I decided that... Never mind. There's no point trying to talk to a dog, anyway."

"What was that?"

"Never mind."

She slammed together the empty packs of yakisoba and roughly threw in the disposable chopsticks. He didn't know what had rubbed her the wrong way, but it seemed her mood had unexpectedly soured, meaning trouble for Ryuuji, which was annoying.

"I have doubts, too," she said. "You understand that, right? That Kitamura-kun might misunderstand our relationship if I try too hard. But...but I'm going to try my best. I'm going to. That's because...basically...you..."

Ryuuji met Taiga's gaze.

Below the parasol under the gloomy sky, Taiga's eyes were bright.

Normally, he could meet that brightness head on, and work painfully hard to indulge Taiga, trying to figure out what she was actually trying to say, or what her true intentions were, or how to fix her mood so she would feel better. Ryuuji was helplessly kindhearted to begin with, but he also shared meals from the same pot as Taiga and had come to think of her as something like a little sister or a comrade at arms. It was also because he knew how clumsy Taiga was and how bad she was at speaking.

But he couldn't do that now.

"But it doesn't have aaaaaanything to do with you!" she said—as usual—and forcefully turned her face away to give him a cold side-eye.

Ryuuji was more than annoyed.

Why is that?

Was it because of the cold? Was it because he was tired? Was it because the yakisoba wasn't any good? Or maybe it was because the countless words of pity their classmates had written on the betting sheets actually hurt him?

Or was it something simpler? Was it because he was always concerned for Taiga, but Taiga always, always, always, always, always, at every available opportunity, said, "I don't care about you, Ryuuji?"

"Oh, is that so?" he said. "Fine. You don't have to try. You're not really motivated anyway."

Or maybe it was because everything that had happened that day sat in his stomach like a stone?

At Ryuuji's harsh voice, the color of Taiga's eyes changed.

"What was that? Who said I'm not motivated? I'm the one who's saying we should practice. I said we're not going home. I'm still going to practice."

"You don't have to push yourself," Ryuuji said. "You don't care about me anyway, right? In that case, you can just give up on the match tomorrow. There isn't any reason for you to try hard. That way Kitamura would know you don't care about me at all, right? And I'll tell Kawashima not to invite Kitamura. And not to invite

Kushieda. Then you'll have something to celebrate, right? Isn't it great that you don't have anything to be upset about? You'll eat convenience store food all summer long. The delivery from the Chinese place in front of the station's pretty good, too."

Taiga became quiet and still as she stared him down. Her eyes glinted. "What do you mean by that?"

"I mean exactly what I said. There's no practice. There's no match. That's fine, right? As long as Kitamura doesn't go to the villa and you don't have to worry about your food, nothing else matters to you, right? Because you don't have any reason or right to complain about where I go or who I go with, right?"

"Oh, I see!" A sound like a laugh spilled from Taiga's colorless lips. "Your true colors have come out! It would have been better if I had noticed from the start! Then I wouldn't have suffered like an idiot!"

"Huh?! What do you mean by 'true colors?!'"

"You *want* to go, don't you?! To 'Kawashima Ami-chan's villa.' It's hilarious! You want to spend your summer with a cute girl?! Of course you would. Spending your precious summer with *me* is such a waste, right?! You should have said from the start you wanted to go! Oh, or maybe, of course! You used me! You used my feelings as an excuse because going around saying you want to go while wagging your tail wouldn't do, so you pretended like you didn't want to go and couldn't do anything about it! How stupid *are* you?!"

"You..." Ryuuji paled from anger. He wanted to scream. Why

did it always have to be like that? Why had he bothered checking the weather with her every day? Why was he practicing flutter kicks with her? Why was he going to a place like this with her when she was going to say stuff like that? *Do you care about me at all?* he wanted to say.

"You girls just don't understand aaaaaanything!"

"That's what I want to say!"

Their voices were like blows, but Ryuuji couldn't understand what Taiga meant. Maybe she didn't understand him either, but still annoyed, still angry, they just continued their exchange.

"It was like that before, too!" Ryuuji shouted. "You're always like that! You always say you don't care about me, and you interpret things as if I did something bad, and you make me out to be the villain and attack me! Why is it always like that?! I'm the one who provoked Kawashima, according to you—what is that?! Why is it I have to be blamed for every little thing?!"

"You're going back to talking about that?!" Taiga snapped.

She got up, kicked the table over, pulled out the parasol, and threw it. The wind whistled. The rain fell by the quiet, deserted poolside.

"Why?! Why won't you understand?! I'm not angry! I'm not! I told you that from the start! It's just that other people misunderstand me." Taiga hit her own heart firmly with her fist. Her voice went hoarse from the screaming.

"You just pretend like you know!" she continued. "I don't want that, it makes me angry! You think I'm angry at *you*?! You want me to say that you're mine?! What... What is that?! Who actually knows what I think of you?! Who's supposed to know?! No one should know because I haven't told anyone! Because I don't know either!"

Ryuuji could barely hear her even though she was shouting. He had gotten stuck in the kiddie pool when dodging the parasol.

Frantically, he crawled out, coughing. "What did you say?!"

"So I'm not going to do that match anymore! Go wherever you want!" Rubbing her eyes, she ran toward the girls' changing room.

How should I know, you idiot? he thought. He half-expected her to do something klutzy, anyway. She'd trip or drop something important, and, in the end, she would have to rely on Ryuuji to help her out. Then, he would sigh and say, "You're such a klutz," and everything would go back to normal. It should have gone back to normal, at least.

Instead, Taiga went home ahead of him in a taxi.

She also didn't come to eat dinner.

Ryuuji didn't go to get her. It seemed he and Taiga had had a real fight.

"I'm not wrong, right?" he asked Inko-chan that night, without meaning to, in the quiet Takasu household.

Inko-chan, almost like a regular parakeet, only said back to him, "Chi chi chi." She wouldn't look Ryuuji in the eyes.

5

J ERK.

Ryuuji woke with a start. The sun was dim. It was five o'clock in the morning.

Waking up from a dream he couldn't really remember, a small flame of anger still burned in Ryuuji's stomach even after sleeping on it. It wasn't the same fury that had riled him up like the day before but rather a low flame that smoldered steadily in his chest.

I was so angry I even woke myself up, Ryuuji thought, which made him even angrier.

He got up, scratched at his head, went to the bathroom, and crossed the cold, wooden floor of the kitchen with his bare feet to wash his hands.

He opened a cupboard, taking out the special, high-quality ham Yasuko had brought back from the bar earlier. It had apparently come from one of her customers. He had intended to save it for a special occasion.

For the time being, he would make the bento.

He was awake now, and if he did nothing, he'd just get annoyed. He didn't care about the match between Taiga and Ami anymore; he'd deal with the weather, the pool, and summer vacation later. For now, he was making bento. Luckily, he had some leftover minced meat, and he could use the chicken leg he had been meaning to cook for that day's dinner. He'd start off with onions, and for the rest of the vegetables, he had eggplant, bell pepper, and shiitake mushrooms. On top of the plentiful and complex side dishes, the main course would be a ham maki roll. He would grill the ham with plenty of butter and a little salt and pepper. Then, he would make a giant, unvinegared maki roll with a sweetened omelet roll and the ham.

I'm going to do it. He was nearly desperate as he opened the refrigerator.

The front door unlocked with a *click*.

"Oh, deary dear?"

Yasuko popped her head inside, looking perplexed. When she saw her son, she grinned. "Why is Ryuu-chan uwp?~" She jumped up and down happily, the strong smell of alcohol wafting around her.

"I woke up, so I thought I could make the bento."

When he poured her a glass of cold buckwheat tea, Yasuko was so drunk she downed it in one go.

"Ahhh, yumm~ Oh, so did you mwake up wiss Taiga-chan yet?~"

"Not yet."

As he diced an onion, Ryuuji shook his head. There was no point in saving face in front of a drunk person.

"Izzat so? Bwut, Ryuu-chan, you getting into a fight with someone, that's a firsht isn't it?"

"Yup."

It was as his mother said.

Embarrassingly, until now Ryuuji had never once raised his voice to anyone or gotten into a real fight. He'd had disagreements before and times where he'd been angry on the inside and smiled to cover it, but this was the first time he'd ever actually shown anyone his anger. It was the worst.

Yasuko exhaled loudly. "Whew! Why're you fwighting, what haaappened? You went to the pwool on such gwood terms..."

And with that, she slumped to the kitchen floor. Ryuuji didn't bother scolding her.

"Taiga said she didn't care what I did, and I got angry I guess."

"Hmmm, is that sooo? Buuut, Ryuu-chan...don't yoo get it? When Taiga-chan shays stuff, she means the opposite, right?"

With splendid knife work, he finely diced the onion on the cutting board in the blink of an eye. His eyes stung. *This is a good onion,* Ryuuji thought.

"Shurely Taiga-chan must have given you a hint, right? Taiga-chan would, definitely, 'cause she likes you, Ryuu-chan. She definitely...cares about...what you do..."

185

CHAPTER 5

Should probably dice one more.

"Maybe she dwoesn't know if she wants to be with you, but if she really hated you, Ryuu-chan, a girl like that'd die before sharing the same plate as you...is what...I think..."

Yasuko's chilly hand softly patted Ryuuji's leg, as if to cheer him up or comfort him.

"Zzz..."

And with that, her hand slumped to the floor. Her snores reeked of alcohol. Yasuko was wasted. Again.

"Jeez, you haven't even taken off your makeup..."

He washed the onion smell off his hands and carried his drunken mother to her bedroom. He laid her on the futon he always put out for her before he went to bed and was hit by a sudden wave of nostalgia.

The smell of perfume coming from Yasuko's chest was the same as it was in the past; it never changed. Like spice, the refreshing and not particularly sweet fragrance suited Yasuko unexpectedly well.

He remembered the dim, single room of a childcare facility in a building and city that was even more rundown than this one. When Yasuko arrived at dawn for him, he was so happy he had jumped into her arms, even though he was sleepy. "Ryuu-chan! Sorry! Sorry!" she would say, and he could smell her perfume.

Even though it was the middle of winter, there had been sweat clinging to the nape of her neck. Whether she was wearing high heels or a miniskirt, she had dashed as fast as she could from the bar to come get Ryuuji.

Even though I tend to forget it, she's definitely my mom, Ryuuji acknowledged. He was old enough to sleep alone now, but Yasuko's sweet words still calmed him.

He put Taiga's bento box next to his own. Despite his anger, and them being in the middle of a fight, in light of Yasuko's words, he would at least make her bento. At any rate, they rarely had such amazing ham, so he intended to make a special gourmet bento.

Am I a mama's boy?

What was wrong with that?

A gentle drizzle continued from the clouded, silver sky.

"Taiga! Hey, wait up!"

He chased the light lavender umbrella, avoiding puddles as he ran. He finally caught up to her under a large Zelkova tree.

"I won't ask you to walk with me! The bento! Just this, take it. 'Cause I worked hard to make it. You didn't eat anything yesterday, right? I put your breakfast into a separate Tupperware, so eat it when you get to school."

"..."

Taiga was strangely silent, and her eyes were full of rage. She was looking down at Ryuuji's feet with a cold expression, as if he were an annoying pebble in her path.

The bento bag he held out to her hung in vain between them.

Then he took a single step, getting closer. He pushed the bento bag into her hand. Droplets of rain splashed on the back of Ryuuji's hand.

"It's raining, huh?"

"..."

"I was really hoping for good weather."

Taiga looked up at Ryuuji's face for just a moment. He searched for words as he kept holding the bento out to her. Not even he knew what he should say to her. But they had already stretched the fight out into overtime, and he wanted to make an excuse for giving her the bento in spite of the argument. *It's not like I'm asking for your forgiveness or anything,* he thought.

"I wanted the weather to clear up since it would be nice if you could come out to the swimming match and..."

Huh.

As he was talking, Ryuuji tipped his head. *Is that right? Do I want Taiga to swim at the match?* Maybe he did want her to go. That's what his mouth had said.

But why?

It was because if he had to go to Kawashima's villa, that would cause trouble.

But couldn't he just tell Ami, "I can't go"? Wouldn't that end the conversation? It wasn't like she would kidnap him.

Even so, he wasn't able to say it. He hadn't said it.

Why didn't he say it before? Why hadn't he said it, and why had he assumed Taiga would win the match for him? Was it because he'd gotten dragged into all this without his consent? Was it because he hadn't had a chance to say anything for himself? He had made excuses. He had assumed she would actually be overbearing. He had assumed she would ignore his feelings. But what exactly were those feelings?

Just as Ryuuji held back the words that would answer his own question, it happened.

"Ah."

Taiga snatched the bento from Ryuuji's hand. "The bento didn't do anything wrong," she said, her eyes cold. "So I'll just take it. But I won't forgive you."

She closed the lavender umbrella forcefully.

A dazzling light shot into Ryuuji's eyes and he closed them tightly.

"I don't know about the match at the pool."

It doesn't matter that you don't know when the weather is like this. Ryuuji finally opened his eyes. He dropped his umbrella in shock.

The silver clouds split for just a moment.

As they watched, the summer rays flowed through relentlessly, warming their skin. The blue sky spread. A drop of light glittered on Taiga's long, upturned eyelashes.

"Hey, you're always around the physical education room, and

don't show your face around the teachers' lounge much. So, I was thinking it might be fun to talk with you. You never even come out with us for drinks."

"Nah, I'm a lightweight."

"Really, what do you do at night? Like on days off? Do you spend time with your girlfriend?"

"I drink protein shakes and go to the gym."

"What, really?! Oh, wow, that's nice. Actually, I've been meaning to go to the gym. I was thinking of starting up yoga or Pilates or something"

"The gym is great! They've got workout machines!"

"They have stuff like hot yoga there, too."

"And then there's weight lifting! Muscle building and power lifting!"

"Uuum... I'm not sure about weight lifting..."

"You know, recently, I've been feeling good! I've really built up my body! What do you think?! What do you think about my back? Or my shoulders? Or my thighs? What do you think?!"

"Y-you're really burly, wooow... Very brawny..."

"Please, I'm 'huge!' Hnghk!"

"Y-you're huge."

"And now say, 'You're ripped'! Right! Hah!"

"You're ripped."

It was no use, she couldn't get through to him. It was impossible. Koigakubo Yuri (twenty-nine and unmarried) shook her head and stood up.

Haruta pointed and laughed. "Oho! Yuri-chan's leaving! How sad!"

Haruta sat next to Ryuuji under the very blue sky. Ryuuji's skin began tingling as he started to quickly warm up.

"But the leading lady hasn't shown up yet today."

"Even though the weather's finally clearing up."

The dazzling midsummer sun blazed down on the students from class 2-C, but even though the pool was inviting, not a single person attempted to go in. They sat in a row by the poolside, saying, "They're late!" or "How much are you betting? On who?"

The tanned and muscled PE instructor had given the students autonomy for the event and seemed quietly absorbed in sunscreen application.

Ryuuji sat, as usual, beside Haruta, Noto, and Kitamura. He wiped the beading sweat from his temple.

Pouting, Haruta poked Ryuuji's shoulders. "Eyy, Takasu. The Palmtop Tiger's definitely coming, right?"

"I've got no clue."

Even to Noto, he couldn't say he thought she wouldn't come because of their fight from the day before. Without his knowing it, the class had cranked up the illegal gambling, and Ami and Taiga's fans were all but starting a rivalry. Supposedly, there was even a tough guy who had bet twenty shares. Everyone who bet on Taiga had said their reasoning was "Because Takasu is brimming with confidence." If they learned Ryuuji was the reason Taiga had abandoned the match, the atmosphere would sour quickly.

Minori was the neutral referee. With a whistle hanging around her neck, she sat quietly on the diving board.

Suddenly, one corner of the spectators stirred. Ryuuji looked up.

"Sooorry! Putting up my hair took a while~"

The ground seemed to shake with voices of admiration. "Whoooooooooooo!"

Even Ryuuji automatically leaned forward and joined in.

Ami had jogged up to them. Her hair was in a beautiful braid, her face was adorable, and her figure was just as perfect as it had always been. But this time...

This time, she was in a jet-black bikini.

"A-a bikini!"

"I'll remember this day until the day I die!"

Her captivating cleavage cast a distinct shadow beneath triangles of cloth that barely looked like they could hold her in. Her stomach was muscular and sculpted, her small, vertical navel exposed. Ami had graduated from angel to alluring demon.

"It's been raining constantly, so I couldn't dry out my regular swimsuit," she said. "No way! What's with everyone?! Don't look at me, that's embarrassing! I-I wonder if I'm breaking any school regulations! I'm a little worried." Ami blushed, pouting her lip as if she were worried.

Couldn't dry her swimsuit? The last pool class was weeks ago. If Ryuuji said that, it would probably be considered boorish. Still, he watched the situation with his mouth half-open like an idiot.

Haruta grabbed his right ear. "That pretty Ami-tan's about to swim in the pool, isn't she?"

Noto grabbed his left. "And she's doing that to take you, Takasu, out to her villa, isn't she?"

"It's always about Takasu, why, why, why, why, why?"

"Why, why, why, why, why is it always about Takasu?"

"Owowowow!"

Envious, they glared at him.

"Jeez, cut it out, guys!" Ryuuji cried, squirmed in pain as they tugged his ears. "I really don't know if there's going to be a match! For starters, if Taiga doesn't come, that's a forfeit."

"Huh? The Palmtop Tiger's not coming? Why?"

"I don't know. This has gotten stupid and out of hand. She didn't care about the match in the first place."

Uwaaaaaah! There was a second commotion, but this was slightly different from the previous one. Ryuuji looked.

"Uwaaah!"

Everyone was astonished.

"That scared me! I thought the Palmtop Tiger finally came up in arms!"

"I totally saw that in Full Metal Jacket!"

Taiga had appeared.

Her hair was in two buns, and her swimsuit was also a bikini. Kind of. It was still the dark blue swimsuit with the faux boob pads. But her small form was surrounded by a variety of flotation devices. She had swim rings in all kinds of sizes blown up and attached to her. She held a kickboard in each hand and carried beach balls and mats tucked under her arms and elbows. It was a smorgasbord of things that would float. They could barely even see her skin.

"W-wait a minute, you! Do you intend to swim like that?!" Ami pointed at Taiga and raised her voice.

Taiga jutted her jaw. "That's right," she said calmly. "Is that not allowed? Is there a ban on 'foreign objects?'"

"Of course there is, right?! If you can't swim, then you forfeit!"

"Is that so? Then take off your swimsuit. Swimsuits are foreign objects, right? Are you planning on swimming naked? Whoa, that's amazing. Though I'm pretty sure you'll be arrested."

"Y-you're twisting your own words!"

"Maybe. Or maybe you're just scared of losing? That's right, if you somehow lost to me when I can't swim, that would be humiliating! That's it, right? I get it."

Ami bit her tongue but immediately recovered her composed smile. "Hmph. Then go ahead and do what you want. I honestly don't think you can swim like that, but at least it's better than you *drowning* like you did before."

"Thank you so much for your concern. You watch yourself, too. Accidents in the water can be scary. You never know what might happen."

The preliminary skirmish ended, they turned away from each other.

With that, Minori stood up. "Well then, let's start the

twenty-five-meter freestyle, one-game match! Amin, give us a word of encouragement!"

"Okay! Let's just have some fun, that's iiit," Ami said.

There was enthusiastic applause and the boys' burgeoning shouts of joy echoed over the poolside.

"Ami-taaan! You're so cuuute!"

"Ami-tan, good luck!"

"I love you!"

"I'm serious!"

"Taiga, can we get a word from you, too?" Minori continued.

"Right. In that case, I'll be blunt. You there! With the bad expression!"

Ryuuji jumped up in surprise at this sudden callout. On the end of Taiga's extended index finger was a flake of seaweed... Upon closer inspection, there were seaweed flakes around her mouth, too. Apparently, she had diligently eaten the seaweed maki he'd made for breakfast.

"Don't let this get to your head," Taiga said. "I didn't come here for you. I just saw this dumb Chihuahua—"

"Who are you calling a dumb *Chihuahua*?!" Ami exclaimed.

"...and her dumb bikini and wanted to embarrass her!"

"What do you mean by 'dumb bikini?!'"

"That's a dumb bikini. It's the first time I've seen an idiot wearing a bikini to the school pool."

"You got a problem with it?! It's pretty!"

"'Pretty' *ugly*."

"What's with the air quotes?!"

With that, Taiga looked away.

Ryuuji's eyes glinted dangerously as he continued watching Taiga. He wasn't trying to cut her swimsuit apart into a bikini with his eyes—he was just surprised. Not by the number of flotation devices on her body, but that Taiga had appeared at all.

He didn't think she'd actually participate. *Because she said that, didn't she? That she wouldn't forgive me. That she didn't care about the match. And now she's saying it's because Ami's in a bikini...*

Leaving Ryuuji in the dust, the peanut gallery applauded just as much as they had for Ami.

"Show me the money!"

"The legend of the strongest continues on!"

"Fight!"

"My master!"

The cries were of a slightly different color but still more than supportive. The pool trembled.

"Shut up, you idiots!" Taiga seemed to have plenty of morale of her own. She bared her teeth, which only encouraged her team to cheer louder.

Then, at Minori's instruction, the two of them began stretching.

"And now...take your positions!"

Ami, with the learned movements of an athlete, bent over at the diving board.

"Hey, can the Palmtop Tiger even dive?!"

"Wouldn't it be better if she went in from the side?!"

"Don't force her to do the impossible!"

Then Taiga stood imposingly on the diving board in a way that made the audience uneasy.

Ami smirked at Taiga. Taiga saw this and looked away, completely ignoring her.

"Ready!"

Minori, with one hand up, put her whistle in her mouth. The crowd went silent. Ami's legs flexed as she gripped the diving board.

Then Taiga looked at Ami's lower torso and pointed unexpectedly. "Oh, look. A hair."

"Huh?!"

Shrrreeeeee! The sharp sound of the whistle reverberated, starting the match. Ami looked up, unsettled and then—

"Fnmuh!"

Huh?!

Taiga threw all the flotation devices, everything she had, at Ami. *Fwump!* Ami wavered and began losing her balance on top of the diving board, her timing completely messed up.

The tiger bared her teeth, and her eyes were like flames. She raised a wooden sword, hidden until now by the flotation devices, in one hand. In her other was a kickboard. Her red mouth open, she jumped on Ami. "There!"

"KYAAAAAA!"

Taiga flew into a soundless, amazing roundhouse kick. She

didn't hit Ami, but the jump was picture perfect. Then she pushed Ami, who had completely lost balance, headfirst into the pool with her pivoting foot. A great column of water rose into the air, and Taiga jumped into the pool after her.

As Ami sank, Taiga clung to her. Were they grabbing at each other? Or fighting?

"What's going on?!"

"It's hot! It's too hot!"

In the middle of the screams and cheers, Ryuuji's mouth was also wide open. *What kind of person does that? Aisaka Taiga. You're... You're okay with this?! You're okay with a match like this?!*

Four white arms thrashed, rapidly slapping the water's surface as the submerged fight continued.

"Pwah!" Taiga emerged first. She clung to the kickboard with a crooked smile that would have sent even the devil running the other way.

Ami emerged, too, her large eyes wide. Hanging from the tip of the wooden sword Taiga held high in one hand was...

"Eee!"

"Like I told you, it's a dumb bikini. And easy to take off. Both you and the bikini are stupid!"

On the tip of Taiga's sword was the top half of Ami's bikini.

"GYAAAAAAAAAAAAAAAAAAAAAAAAAAAAAAAAAAA AAAAAAAA!" Ami shrieked.

"WHOAAAAAAAAAAAAAAAAAAAAAAAAAAAAAAAA AAAAAAAAAA!" the boys roared.

Hiding her exposed chest with her hands, Ami's angelic mask was completely gone. She looked desperately for her swimsuit, but Taiga had it.

"There! If you want it, go and get it!"

Taiga waved the wooden sword as if she were casting a fishing line and flung the wet swimsuit in the air. *Splat.* It landed on the fence behind the starting line.

"I can't believe this! I can't believe it! I caaaaaan't!" Ami's crying and fussing did nothing to change the reality of the situation. She was hiding her chest with her hands but couldn't move one step forward from where she was.

Taiga took her chance. Holding firmly onto the kickboard, she kicked, skimming across the water at an unbelievable speed.

"Whaaa! This is definitely going to be a win for the Palmtop Tiger!"

"Damn it, you coward!"

"I'll save Ami-tan!"

Naturally, Ami's fans weren't going to stay silent while Taiga gained more and more of a lead. They dashed to get Ami's bikini back to her.

"No way!"

"Sorry, Ami-chan, but we're not going to let you move!"

The Taiga fans began running. The two hostile forces collided, and the bikini top landed in the hands of...

"Oh, wait a sec, let me smell it."

"Let me touch it, just even for a second."

The boys. They began trying to grab it from each other until someone said, "We're all in this together! I don't care about the money or anything, I just want to keep seeing Ami-tan like that!"

Yeaaah! They all looked over at Ami in agreement.

Ami, her pale, bare skin exposed, sank into the water to her chin and yelled, "Hurry and give it back! You idiots!"

"Seriously, you horn dogs! Hand it over! Hey, Ami-chan, pass!"

"Thanks, Maya-chan!"

Maya, who had somehow cut through the group of boys, nabbed the swimsuit and threw it toward Ami.

"Ami-taaan! I'll save you now!"

"I want to be near her, too!"

"Like I'd let you! The money, the swimsuit, and Ami-tan's white skin are all mine!"

"I'm going to be the one to plant my flag!"

"Nooo!"

The idiots, brains clouded by perversity, were aiming for all sorts of things as they jumped into the pool together, following the swimsuit. Minori fervently blew her whistle.

"Hey, don't approach the athlete! I'll have you arrested for sexual harassment! Gah! Seriously! Listen to me!"

But no one was listening.

"I got Ami-tan's swimsuit!"

"Give it to me!"

"Ami-tan, are you okay?! You're not hurt?!"

"Eek! Don't come near me, don't come near me, don't come near me!" Ami bellowed.

"A-Ami-tan?"

"You sounded so scary just then!"

"No way ♥. Maybe you misheard me?" she said.

The girls signaled to each other, their angry expressions directed at the boys.

"We won't forgive you!"

"Get a hold of yourselves!"

"You sexual harassers!"

The girls jumped in to forcibly pull the boys away from Ami and out of the pool.

Haruta and Noto also jumped in, too.

"I want in!" Haruta shouted.

"How can I stand by for something as fun as this!" Noto said.

And they pushed Kitamura in with them, with a, "You come, too!"

Only Ryuuji, stunned, was left behind. His eyes met those of the person who was trying her best to stay out of the bikini-stealing ring but had a central role in the fight.

And Ami, even in a time like this, was grinning at Ryuuji.

"Tee-hee, do you want to see?~"

"You idiot!"

She gently shifted the hands that were hiding her chest. How could she be so calm at a time like this?

Behind her, like a strange bird, the bikini flew above Ami's head.

"Pass it here!"

"Don't give it to a boy!"

The girls passed Ami's swimsuit around, back and forth, like an amazing water polo play.

"Ami-chan, it's coming! Pass!"

"Yes, thank you!"

Finally, the swimsuit returned to Ami's hands. Ami sank deep into the pool for a moment, and when she raised her head back up, her swimsuit was back on. She went into an all-out front crawl right away.

The peanut gallery all focused their eyes on Ami. Only Ryuuji was looking at Taiga. *Is Taiga actually swimming? Is she going forward without drowning? Is she being a klutz, is she running into trouble?* Even though they had fought the day before, he couldn't take his eyes off her.

"Whoa!" His exclamation was thick in his throat as he raised a cry.

Taiga had been struggling forward, but the next moment, her small body sank into the water. Ryuuji stood; no one else had noticed. He ran from the poolside and jumped in. With all his strength, he swam.

He could only see Taiga's arms slapping the water's surface. There was no mistaking that she was drowning. *But she has a kickboard, so how?! Why?!* he wondered as he swam, but there was no way to tell without asking Taiga herself.

"Taiga! Are you okay?! You're doing a pretty good job at drowning!"

Holding her, he brought her face up out of the water, but Taiga desperately flapped her arms and legs. Even though she was drowning, she tried to tear herself from Ryuuji's hands. Her face twisted in anguish, and her eyes were red with tears.

"Let go!" she cried. "Get away!"

"I can't let go of you when you're like this!"

"Shut up, I hate yooou... owowowowowow!"

"What's wrong?"

"M-my leg's cramped up!"

"It's karma for cheating!"

The match was done. Ryuuji tried to signal that to Minori.

"Heeey, I can still do it! The kickboard, the kickboard!"

Even though she was grimacing and coughing, Taiga slapped away Ryuuji's hand and latched onto the kickboard once again. She pulled on her apparently cramped right foot and forced herself to stretch it.

"Y-you're doing it?!"

Taiga stared straight ahead. "I'm doing it!"

"But you're—"

You just said you didn't care. You just said all you wanted to do was embarrass the dumb Chihuahua. If you were just embarrassing her, you've done more than enough. Ryuuji was at a loss for words.

Taiga stared hard at him and said, "You're happy, right?!"

"Wha...?"

"Don't 'wha' me! Your master's doing her best for you. Be happy, you slow dog!"

Ryuuji didn't have time to say anything else before Taiga began trying to swim again. He just grabbed Taiga's waist and pushed her forcefully forward.

"Then go!" he said. "I'll wag my tail for you or whatever you want!"

Using the momentum he'd given her, Taiga restarted her flutter kicks and smoothly resumed swimming.

But everyone had jumped into the pool. The swimsuit theft had spawned an all-out boys vs. girls battle. They were tossing each other into the pool, splashing water everywhere.

Then, someone was thrown forcefully in right beside Ryuuji.

"Huuuh?! Ryu—Ryuuji?!"

"Gwah, blergh, burble..."

Their elbow, or knee, or something made a clean hit on Ryuuji's head. The strength left his entire body all at once, and he felt himself sinking. Just as his vision began fading, he saw Taiga, who had apparently turned around in surprise at the splash. She looked at him with her round eyes. The noises of the pool became rowdier, and he knew no one else had noticed.

"Ryuuji! Ryuujiii!" Taiga's voice became more and more muffled, and his breath... Wait, no, he *could* breathe.

His unmoving body was pulled up by something strong and put...onto a kickboard?

"Someone... Hey, someone...glug, glug...*cough!* Damn it!"

He could hardly call the small hands that held onto him strong. But Ryuuji couldn't move his own arms, and his vision was black, and he was definitely half-unconscious. He couldn't move; he couldn't even raise his cheek from where it was stuck to the kickboard.

The kickboard rocked. Ryuuji began slipping, cold water flooding his mouth. Right before he was about to choke, small hands firmly went around his head. They were warm and gentle as they supported his chin. The water that touched his skin tickled as it flowed evenly around him. They were probably moving forward very quickly.

Finally, he was able to open his eyes a crack. Everything around him was rocking even more intensely than he'd thought. Taiga was crying.

"Weeeh!"

But she kept her arm around Ryuuji's neck. Half-sinking, with one hand desperately gripping the kickboard, she paddled. She was still heading toward the finish line. Even though it had come to this, she couldn't let the words *I give up* out of her mouth. Even though she was crying like a baby, she wouldn't lose.

But something moving at great velocity began closing in on her...something like a dolphin, picking up more and more speed.

Someone shouted, "Why are Takasu and Tiger both on the kickboard?!"

"Waaah, they're being left in the dust!"

"Takasu, why you!"

"Go, go, Ami-taaan!"

207

Ryuuji couldn't argue. Still half-unconscious, he saw the dolphin easily cut through the water. In the middle of the hoarse screams and cheering, she easily breezed past the awkward, two-person kickboard team.

"Goal! Justice wins!" she said.

At the same time, the small hands cradling the kickboard lost the last of their strength. "Oof."

Cheers rose up then immediately fell silent.

Someone muttered, "Huh, do you think Takasu and Tiger are drowning?"

Yes, we are.

We're drowning.

Actually, Taiga, with an already injured foot and having used all of her strength, had left Ryuuji and the kickboard on the surface as she sank.

"Whaaat?!" Ami shrieked.

SPLASH! A large, abnormally buff mass of muscle jumped into the pool.

Kuro-muscle, who was responsible for supervising them, was in trouble now.

"Cough...cough, cough, cough, cough!"

Taiga was on her knees and coughing painfully.

Next to her, Ryuuji was still half-unconscious. He was limp, laid out on the ground by the pool and couldn't lift a finger. He could hear someone far away asking, "Takasu, are you okay?!"

"He's breathing!"

"Okay, let's get him to the nurse's office!"

No, I'm fine. Finally, he got a lungful of oxygen. His dizziness began clearing. Ryuuji attempted to rise onto his elbow to reassure everyone.

"Don't touch hiiiiiim!"

In his narrow field of vision, he knew something outrageous was happening. Her hair limp and her eyes red, Taiga gave them a terrible look as she straddled Ryuuji like a tiger.

"You're all idiots, idiots, idiots, *idioooooots*! Why didn't you notice? Why didn't you help? You morons, don't come near him! Get away! I hate all of you! Get away, get away!"

She had snapped; she had completely snapped. Kuro-muscle's hot bod couldn't compare to Taiga's hot anger, and he flinched. The girl with the name of a tiger had lost it. Her growling smacked of the wild, and her shouts were mixed with tears.

"Ryuuji is miiiiiiiiiiiiine! No one touch him! Ryuuji is *miiiiiine*!"

Everyone in class 2-C was silent.

The pool was silent.

The sky was blue, and the sun was hot.

"Hm? Huh?"

Taiga realized the meaning of the words she had unexpectedly yelled.

I'll pretend to still be unconscious for a little while longer. Ryuuji closed his eyes firmly and let his consciousness slip away.

It may have been because he was literally unconscious, but Ryuuji was smiling slightly. He was happy; his feelings were clear.

What Taiga just said made him happy. He'd been happy the whole time.

The time when Taiga had taken his wrist and hidden him behind her back.

The time when she said she didn't want to let him go to Ami's villa.

The time when she said she would keep practicing even as it rained.

And, also, probably the time when Taiga was angry when she saw him with Ami.

He hadn't realized it until now, but he'd been happy. So even though she had ignored him and he had been annoyed and they had fought, now, he was smiling.

Taiga said to be happier, right? I'm happy, I was happy from the start. He smiled.

"Eek?!"

"T-Takasu's plotting something!"

"Everyone hide!"

"It was like hell!"

BAM!

"H-hey...are you okay?"

Her head on the table, Taiga only raised her eyes as she glared at Ryuuji. There was so much bloodlust in her gaze that it practically dripped down her cheeks.

"Don't ask if I'm okay," she said, her low voice pitiful.

It had been two weeks since the last day of swimming classes and the end-of-term exams. Even for the Palmtop Tiger, it had all been too much.

They were at their usual non-smoking sofas in their usual family restaurant. Although their end-of-term ceremonies had ended, and it was lunch, it wasn't crowded. Maybe it was because it was a weekday?

In any case, it was probably a good thing there weren't other customers watching as Taiga kicked her feet like a child and verbally abused Ryuuji.

"It's your fault, you dog! Because of you, I've had nothing but horrible experiences! Menu!"

Ryuuji handed her the menu.

Indeed, the last few days had been difficult for Taiga. "Ryuuji is miiiiiine," had apparently convinced the class that Taiga and Ryuuji were a thing.

No matter how much Taiga denied it or made a fuss, they refused to believe otherwise. In the end, even Kitamura and Minori were saying things like "It was a long time coming," and "You've finally sealed it." They may have been joking, but they still said it.

"Have you made up your mind?~ Hee hee, you're so steamy even in the early afternoon!"

Like that.

"Minorin!" Taiga said. "I told you to stop already! You're terrible!"

"Sorry, sorry! It's a joke, a joke! Don't cry, don't cry!"

Minori, who had gotten to the restaurant one step ahead of them, patted Taiga's head with a bowl. She was in her pale orange waitress uniform.

"What a mess," she said, looking at Ryuuji.

"You're the one who made her cry."

"Did I? Ha ha!"

Don't laugh. Go do your work. He couldn't say it out loud. They weren't close enough for him to joke with her like that.

Ryuuji looked quietly at Minori's smile and thought, *She really is dazzling.* He couldn't even look at her directly. It filled his chest with a mysterious buzz. He couldn't pass it off as the completely unqualified, unrequited love of before. He *was* still in love with Minori, but...

That reason he was doubting himself was because of the grumbling person before him right now. It was because of that tiny person who was telling Minori off for rubbing her head. Since the incident at the pool, Ryuuji had been slightly confused.

First off, he was happy about her saying, "Ryuuji is miiiiine." It was true, and lying to himself wouldn't help. And the feeling was mutual, to an extent: He liked Taiga. If he didn't like her, he wouldn't take care of her. And he himself had said that a tiger and dragon came as a set.

But he didn't just like her like a guy liked a girl, did he? Maybe it was just friendship or brotherly love. There were a lot of other emotions like that, weren't there? That's probably what this was. *Whatever it is, Taiga is Taiga, and liking her like that is fine,* he decided.

The problem was Taiga.

What had Taiga been feeling when she declared "Ryuuji is miiiiiine"? *Could it be...?* Ryuuji couldn't help wondering. As a result, his stomach was in knots, and he couldn't feel at ease.

"Wait! I told you to stop that, didn't I?! You broke dog!" Taiga shook him violently, as if trying to produce money from his pockets.

Someone at the next table said, "Excuse me, can we order?" and Minori had to rush over to do her job.

"What is it with you?" Taiga was clearly in a bad mood.

"Huh?!"

A dubious presence drifted into the toxic atmosphere between them.

"You were looking at me just now. What? What is it? Do you have something to complain about?"

"N-no. I wasn't looking at you."

"You were! You're the worst! You've been ogling me since lunch and imagining unspeakable things, haven't you?"

"What?! Why would you think that?!"

"…"

"Don't ignore me!"

Agitated, he clambered to his feet—just as people he recognized walked in.

"Yo! Did we keep you waiting?"

"Takasu-kun, sorry for making you wait! Oh, sorry for making this little one wait, too."

Ami, as if it were natural, sat herself down next to Ryuuji at the four-seater table. Then, out of necessity, Kitamura sat next to Taiga.

"What's wrong, Aisaka?" Kitamura asked. "Why are you gulping down your water? You're going to get a fountain drink anyway, aren't you?"

Taiga turned away, still guzzling her water. She couldn't bring herself to look at him. The ice in the bottom of her glass tumbled against the tip of her nose.

"Ahhhhhhhhh! Taiga! You're spilling it!"

"Uhhh." Like a child, Taiga let water dribble over her chin.

Ryuuji quickly pulled out his pocket tissues and wiped the table, cleanly and methodically mopping up anything that might spill onto Taiga's lap.

There! He nodded amicably.

Ami nestled up to his arm as though to fawn on him. "Hey, Takasu-kun, why did you call me here? Oh, maybe it's because of the villa? In that case, next time we meet up, we can start planning the trip."

"I called you here, you dumb Chihuahua."

"Huh?!"

Taiga turned her body completely to the right to keep from touching Kitamura, but the left half of her impish face was the color of cherry blossoms. "I decided I'm going, too. To your villa. Because I lost at your match. I'll be in trouble without Ryuuji to take care of me. Ryuuji's mother can fend for herself, but she can't look after me. So there's no helping it! I'm going with him. Deal with it!"

"Huh? Wait a second!" Ami exclaimed. "How can you suggest something so selfish?!"

In actuality, it was Kitamura who had suggested taking Taiga to Ami's villa, and he had asked them to try to get Ami to agree.

"I'm also planning on going, and Kushieda is going, so in that case, don't you think everyone should come along?" Kitamura had said. Ryuuji and Taiga still couldn't figure out what his true motives were. Still, it was a chance for Taiga to go on a trip with Kitamura. Taiga had hesitantly agreed on the condition that if Ami said no outright, they'd back off.

Kitamura, enjoying himself, pushed up his glasses and spread out a calendar he had drawn with freehanded lines on loose-leaf paper.

"Good!" he said. "So then, let's choose a schedule. First, I have a student council retreat here, and softball club retreat here, a practice match here..."

"Y-Yuusaku?! What are you deciding that on your own for?"

"Hey, Kushieda, are you free now? We're deciding the trip schedule."

"Oh! Let me see?! Ummm, I have club at the same time as Kitamura here, and here, and I'm in work shifts all through here, so I think this time might be the best."

"I don't have anything in particular. I might need to visit some graves, but I can do that any time. Taiga, you don't have anything either, right?"

"No. I wouldn't go on a family trip even if it killed me."

"In that case, let's make it this week—"

"W-w-wait! Wait a second! Why are you making these decisions about my villa?! Why is everyone else calling the shots?!" Ami stood, raising her voice. She snatched up Kitamura's calendar.

Looking up at Ami's flushed face, Taiga whispered, in her usual monotone, "Is the villa too small?"

"Huh?! Of course not! My parents pay a ton of money for it!"

"Ahhh, so it's so run down you don't want anyone to see."

"Of course not! It's super big and pretty and the scenery is great, and it's *waaay* better than your condo!"

"Then show us."

"Wha...?"

"Why not? Show me. I want to go, too."

Ami opened her mouth, at a loss for words for a moment. She frowned sullenly. "Seriously?"

The angel was gone. Ami thumped into the sofa as she sat down hard and threw the calendar back onto the table. "*Fiiine.*

I'll do it. Gladly. I'll blow your mind with my super celebrity villa. Even if I say no, you'll still find a way to come anyway, right?"

Taiga smirked, lightly contorting her lips. "Good."

Kitamura laughed. "Ami, this summer seems like it'll be a lot of fun," he whispered, but Ami either hadn't heard him or pretended not to listen. Either way, she didn't reply.

They returned to their conversation about the schedule.

"Oh. I see," Ami said, her voice thick with laughter. What didn't kill her just made her stronger. She really wasn't a normal person. "Aisaka-san. You have anxiety about being away from Ryuuji? Right? You're thinking I'm going to steal him so you want to come along? After all, 'Ryuuji is miiiiiine'...right? ♥"

Oh no, this is dangerous, Ryuuji looked at Taiga. Ami had practically body slammed a land mine—she wouldn't escape unscathed.

But when Taiga raised her head, her expression was unexpectedly calm. "Right. I guess I'll clarify that."

She lifted her chin, her posture perfect. She was facing everyone rather than just facing Ami. "You know, how should I put this? I feel like no one's going to approve."

Ryuuji was uneasy. *What's with her? What's she trying to say?*

"I admit it. I saw this dumb Chihuahua and Ryuuji together, and I was super angry about it."

Even Minori, who finally had a moment to spare, had heard and almost dropped her bowl at Taiga's confession. Kitamura pushed up his glasses. Ami was on the verge of saying something but held her breath.

Somehow, Ryuuji knew Taiga was about to say something monumental. Her face was that serious.

"I said Ryuuji is mine. I won't ask you to pretend that didn't happen. I do really feel that way. Because that's...basically..." Taiga quietly closed her eyes, placing her white hands on her chest.

Nobody could speak, and Ryuuji felt like his heart was about to jump out of his mouth. No way. No way, why would you say something like that in a place like this? If you're going to say something like that, we should talk it over alone together and, in a calmer, more normal—

"Uh..."

Taiga opened her beautiful, glittering eyes, staring intently at Ryuuji. Ryuuji was so unsettled, he backed away as far as he could go. Then the following words issued steadily from her rosy lips: "Because he's my dog."

"Huh?"

"He's my dog. I thought I didn't care what he did with other people, but that's not the case. For example, as his owner, I can't let my own dog get excited and pant and breathe all over an old man I don't know. What if he started humping his back or something?!"

Without thinking, Ryuuji sank down, down, down into the sofa. He didn't know whether he was exhausted or relieved, or... *Well, it's fine. It's fine, really.*

"What's with that face? What were you expecting?" Taiga stared Ryuuji down with a venomous, teasing smile.

"I wasn't expecting anything." Ryuuji righted and recomposed himself, and dropped his eyes to the calendar. Summer vacation began the following day. He would forget all the dull things and have a good time. *I'll have fun,* he thought.

He would have fun, even if he spent the majority of his vacation with Taiga, who he was always with. The good times they had together would continue through summer vacation.

Ryuuji felt a cold sensation against his leg. Under the table, Ami had her fingertip on his knee. "What?"

Ami smirked. In a quiet whisper that no one else could hear, she said, "Too bad it's not just the two of us. But don't worry, we'll have lots of chances to be alone." Her profile was gentle and angelic; there was no apparent evil in her expression. No one noticed, and his heart jumped slightly.

"Good! Then let's decide on this day for the trip!" Kitamura said.

They applauded.

And so, the curtain closed on the first semester of Takasu Ryuuji's second year of high school.

Afterword

I WENT TO A POPULAR fortune-telling website that has a reputation for accuracy. The fortune I got was, "An exceptionally dull person. If they find something they like, they'll continue to eat nothing but that." It's accurate.

Hello, I'm Takemiya Yuyuko.

Everyone I meet tells me that if I eat nothing but tarako spaghetti, it'll poison my body (and my fortune), so I've been a little more careful lately about making sure to have sides, too.

And by that, I mean fried chicken from the freezer. For each meal, I have four pieces (two minutes in the microwave), but the brand I like apparently has seventeen pieces per bag, so the fourth time around I get five pieces.

I look so, so forward to the days I get to have five pieces that I wake up early. "Oh, today's the day I get five pieces~" Then I'm wide awake! Vegetables? Yeah, right, vegetables...

Incidentally, even though I've added a side, I haven't decreased the amount of spaghetti I eat. I mean, it's been hot lately, and if I get heat exhaustion, my work will suffer.

As a member of society, I've taken responsibility for managing my well-being. I diligently eat for two.

So, to everyone who has picked up *Toradora!* Volume 3, I sincerely, sincerely thank you! Did you enjoy it?

I usually have a narrow focus when it comes to writing about boobs, but this time I feel like I had a missile in my hands. I'm fine, really. My romcom gun still has butt bullets and all kinds of other bullets besides, so I've got more where that came from. I still haven't expended all my boob bullets, so I won't hold back on the barrage going forward.

I would be very grateful if you continued with me in the next installment. Please, please do!

Incidentally, do you readers think I can't swim? I can swim. Or rather, I don't sink. I'm the type who can float naturally on top of the water when I relax. Actually, if I try to dive, my butt goes up and floats, so I feel like I'm about to do a handstand on the bottom.

I've really gotten into *Animal Crossing* as of late. Unimpressive, I know. Every day, I twirl my spaghetti with my right hand while my left hand manipulates my stylus every which way. I pick up my fried chicken with my tongue. That's a lie.

I wish it were a lie.

Because I do nothing but play games. I haven't exercised in ages; but in the game, I'm running around the village, collecting bugs, fishing, digging up fossils, and I've got a super active life. So, it's fine.

But something bad that's come out of my serious gaming is that my chronic stiff shoulders and backaches have gotten a lot worse. My massage therapist told me, "You're in the worst condition. You already have frozen shoulder (and you're getting fatter and fatter)." It's no wonder I can't raise my shoulder. My massage therapist would massage and massage me, but I would come back in the same terrible condition every time. "I play games too much," I'd smile and say. I can't imagine how futile my massage therapist must feel.

I was addicted. Days went by where I couldn't communicate my sincerity to the animals of the village. "Hey, Yuyuko-shi~, I want ____," they'd say. And so, because of that unexpected request, I could only look desperately for the object they begged for, somehow get it, and give it to them. Then they would say something like, "Uwah, thank you! You're amazing Yuyuko-shi~" They would smile adoringly at me, and the next day, throw the object in the trash. Any normal person would be hurt. Then, even though the animal itself threw it away, the next day or so after that, it would say, "Hey, Yuyuko-shi, I want ____ (the same thing)." Like, *what?!*

Feeling a little empty, I thought of trying another game. What I mean is *that* game. I'm talking about *Brain Age*.

First, I checked my brain age. I took a formal test where you answer questions by speaking out loud. You must be thinking, "You got a super old age, and you're about to make that into a joke, aren't you, Yuyuko?" You'd be wrong.

Because my voice was too soft, or maybe for some other reason, it didn't even detect me.

Well, lately, I haven't been talking to people in real life. It seems I've forgotten how to use my voice.

It's fine. Really. Well, I'm going to the village to catch some bugs. Because in this world, I can wave a net around even if I have a frozen shoulder.

And so, I am very grateful for everyone who has stayed with me through to the end! Coming up next is *Toradora!* Volume 4! I would be so, so grateful if you would continue to support the next installment. And thank you to everyone who has sent letters with their reactions! I read them all with the editorial department's Manager-san. It's encouraging!

I also got comments from Kurafuji Sachi-sensei who is illustrating the serialization of *Our Dear Tamura-kun* in *Dengeki Comic Gao!* Thank you very much!

And then, Yasu-sensei, Manager-sama, thank you for taking care of me this time, as well. Let's keep shooting a barrage of boob bullets from the romcom gun!

—Takemiya Yuyuko

NICE TO MEET YOU, I'M KURAFUJI SACHI.
I WAS CHOSEN TO DRAW AN ILLUSTRATION TO CELEBRATE
THE PUBLICATION OF *TORADORA!* VOLUME 3! THANK YOU
VERY MUCH!
I'VE ALSO HAD THE HONOR OF ILLUSTRATING ANOTHER
BOOK TAKEMIYA AND YASU HAVE WORKED ON TOGETHER
CALLED OUR DEAR TAMURA-KUN. IT'S SERIALIZED IN
DENGEKI COMIC GAO! IF YOU ARE INTERESTED, PLEASE
READ AND ENJOY IT.
EXPERIENCE TAMURA-KUN'S BITTERSWEET LOVE AGAIN!
NOW WITH THE HELP OF THE PALMTOP TIGER!!

KURAFUJI-SAN'S ILLUSTRATION on the previous page was splendid, wasn't it?! She's illustrated Matsuzawa and Souma and Taiga wonderfully! It's kind of moving! [tears] She also works on the manga version of *Our Dear Tamura-kun*, which is serialized in *Dengeki Comic Gao!* Please take a look at it.

Well then. From here on out is Yasu's deplorable afterward. (lol)

Long time no see. I'm Yasu. I'm in charge of illustrating *Toradora!* We're finally on the third volume. Because *Tamura-kun* was only two volumes, this really means a lot to me, and I'm excited about it. My doubts have finally flown away. I'll focus on the present and work hard.

Because of the strange heat wave, I feel like my body temperature has been steadily rising every day. I can't leave my apartment's AC, and I'm becoming weaker and weaker by the moment. Speaking of which, a little while ago I got hold of a certain handheld game made by Nintendo. I've been occasionally playing it and coming across some animals. I dig holes to make the residents get stuck, make them fall into pits, chop down all the trees—it's really fun. The residents of my "Yasuken Town" indiscriminately flee, and it's become a ghost town. I did it! It's a really... revealing...game.

Messages to the people who helped me—

- **To Takemiya Yuyuko-sensei:** You always let me read your lovely novels. I'm happy whenever I can help even a little by drawing illustrations. I'm going to give it my all!
- **To the editorial department:** I'm so sorry for waiting until the very last moment and putting you in a dangerous position this time. I am really sorry. Without my manager's precise instructions, it would have been even more precarious (even though it was already bad enough as it was...). Really, thank you very much. I'll do my best.
- **To Ishi-san, who helped me, and also Oyama-sensei:** Thank you for everything! Let's work hard together!
- **To the people who bought this book and visited my homepage:** As always, thank you so much! I'm still inexperienced, so I'll do the best I can!

With that, I pray we meet again in Volume 4. Thank you very much.